I0543070

The Island
Now and Forever 2

TAMMY DENNINGS MAGGY

Copyright for this version
© 2018 Tammy Dennings Maggy and Sassy Vixen Publishing
LLC
Originally published 2012
Cover Design: Maria @ Steamy Designs
All cover art and logo design copyright 2018 by Sassy Vixen
Publishing LLC
All rights reserved.
ISBN: 0-9861543-9-3
ISBN-13: 978-0-9861543-9-3

DEDICATION

This book is dedicated to those in search of their
Always and Forever.
Listen to your heart.
Your soulmate is out there calling out to you.

CONTENTS

ACKNOWLEDGMENTS

Many people cheered me on while writing this book and the others in the series. Without their support, I never would have taken the chance and sent my work in to Siren for consideration. Now, with the re-release of The Island, I've moved into a new realm for me and my characters. By including the paranormal elements, I hoped to show that there are forces out there greater than what we can see, feel, and touch. Whether you believe in them or not, they're still there watching, waiting, and, yes, giving you a little nudge from time to time.

For me, these nudges came in the form of many fabulous authors and friends who've stood by me every step of the way, offering encouragement, laughter, and friendships that I will cherish forever. Several fellow Siren authors have helped me more than they will ever know just by being themselves. Heather Rainier and Tymber Dalton never tired answering questions from a "newbie," and because of them, I kept working and plotting away when I thought I couldn't fit writing in my hectic, busy schedule.

My Moon Sisters Tara Stevens, Amber Lea Easton, and Madison Sevier have been my sounding boards, offering much-needed advice, laughter, and shoulders to cry on when I didn't think things were moving in the right direction. Most of all, they showed me by example how to live my dream of being a writer while balancing the challenges of real life without going completely insane.

A special dedication to one of my besties from high school, Donna Langmaid. At the beginning of July 2018, Heaven called her home. Lady Fate needed another Guardian Angel to help her watch over those of us here in the Earthly Realm. Donna's smile and laughter brought me through many tough moments even though we were two thousand miles apart. She faced all of her health issues head on and will always be my inspiration to embrace every moment. I love you, Babe!

Finally, I owe everything else to my husband. Without his unwavering support of my writing, there wouldn't be any finished manuscripts, just notebooks filled with ideas, plot points, and characters still screaming to have their stories told. Liam is my muse, my knight in shining armor, and my heart and soul. With him, I finally found my own happy ever after. For all you do and for so much more, I love you, honey! You are my always and forever, and I'm thankful for finally finding you in this lifetime. My cup truly runneth over.

CHAPTER 1

"Thirteen years is a long time to hold a grudge, Jake."

Jacob squeezed his wife's hand and brought it to his lips. "That's just it. I let that part of my past go once and for all when you came into my life. My life with Julia is something I would rather keep in the past. It's got nothing to do with us or our family now."

Both looked to the twins strapped safely in their infant carriers secured in the cushioned passenger seats between them. The babies had dozed off as soon as the plane reached cruising altitude. Quinn shook her head, incredulous over her children's ability to sleep anytime or anywhere. "If it wasn't for Julia Santos pushing you over the edge, we might never have met when we did."

Jacob smiled. "Have you been remembering more about—?"

"The Island? Yes. All those instances of déjà vu we've been having? Those are real memories. We *were* there together on that island thirteen years ago falling head over heels for each other."

He opened his mouth to tell her about his flashbacks and paused. He caught a sudden movement out of the corner of his eye. Jacob smiled as one of the stewardesses approached them, pushing a small serving cart before her.

"Mr. and Mrs. Hartley? The captain has reached cruising altitude. You can now move about the cabin as you wish. Can I get anything more for the two of you? Mr. Eischer keeps the jet fully stocked, including several of these chilling in the refrigerator." She produced two teething rings, one pink and one blue.

Jacob laughed and took them from her. "Steve knows these little monsters well. Both of them have been cutting teeth this week. Once they wake up, they'll be in full chomping mode!"

Quinn thanked the stewardess and tucked a teething ring next to each of her children's little fingers. Even asleep, they instinctively brought the rings to their mouths and suckled. "How about you contact Julia as soon as we land and set up a meeting for tonight? I'm sure Steve will be more than happy to entertain his only godchildren for a few hours. He's been waiting for us to make this trip since last year. How much do you wanna bet he's converted one of his guest rooms into a full-on nursery for Stephanie and Daniel?"

He leaned in and kissed each little forehead. "That would be a sucker bet and you know it."

She nodded. "Just as sure as I am he would have done it over any of our objections."

She sat back in her seat and rubbed his thigh. "Babe, what's wrong?"

The smile left his face as he ran his fingers through his long brown hair, pulling it back into a ponytail. "Do you really think I should meet with her tonight?" He was worried seeing Julia again would bring up way too much pain from his past. He didn't want to live through that again, especially now that everything was going so well for him and Quinn. He had been in full-on worry mode from the moment he received the letter from Dr. Carmen Hall, Julia's longtime girlfriend.

"She sounded excited to find you again. Seems to me if seeing you would help Julia's therapy, we should at least try."

"Carmen said no strings, but the Julia I knew always had an ulterior motive."

Carmen had gone into great detail about how she found Jacob after all of these years. Apparently, it had been by chance. The doctor had attended a medical seminar in San Francisco and had run across newspaper articles mentioning a hotshot veterinarian named Quinn Hartley. The feature stories had been about the expansion of the veterinary specialty center where Quinn and her friend Sarah were on staff. The paper had done a special piece on Quinn and how she juggled her career and the twins. Carmen had taken a chance and sent a letter to Jacob in care of Quinn's hospital, hoping she had found the same Jacob Hartley she knew from many years before.

Julia had been in therapy for the last twelve years to work through emotionally and physically painful issues from her childhood. A critical part of the process for her was to confront those who had hurt her in the past and to try to make amends with those she herself had hurt. Carmen mentioned that Julia had put off locating him because she wasn't ready to face that part of her past yet. Now she was, and both of the women were hopeful Jacob would be willing to at least hear Julia out. No strings attached.

Quinn picked up the letter again and scanned through it. "It says here Julia will be in Vegas for a meeting with Steve concerning sculptures for his casinos. In fact, she arrives this afternoon, but Carmen won't be able to join her for a few more days. It would be nice to meet with both of them over dinner, but if we put it off it may never happen. So, I would say the timing's perfect. The sooner you both see each other again, the faster she can move on with her own therapy and recovery and the sooner you can say you've officially let go of that part of your life. You're under no obligation to forgive her. All she is asking for is a few moments of your time."

Quinn got up from her own seat and moved to sit in Jacob's lap, holding him tight. "Don't worry anymore about how you're going to feel seeing her again. I'll be there right by your side the whole time. Sounds to me from what Carmen wrote in her letter Julia really needs to square things with you now."

Jacob snorted. "I know Eric would like to square a few things with her himself."

Quinn pulled back and stared at him. Her eyes never failed to pull him in and calm him down. It was their blue-green shade, just like the color of the ocean, that gave him such comfort. When he gazed into her eyes, he knew he was safe and could do anything with her by his side. "It's not about your brother. It's about a woman trying to make amends so she can find happiness in her life. You found yours, Jake. Shouldn't Julia get the same chance?"

He reached up and tucked a few stray hairs behind her left ear. "Well, when you put it that way, how can I say no?"

She rested her forehead against his and smiled. It was the very same smile that had stolen his heart the moment he laid eyes on her. "I'm glad you finally see things my way! Besides, I'm curious about the woman you nearly killed yourself over."

He groaned and buried his head on her shoulder.

"And I would like to thank her."

He lifted his head and searched her face. "Thank her for what?"

"If she hadn't been such a shit back then, I never would've found you on the Island."

He released the air he had been holding in his lungs while waiting for her to answer and smiled. "If it wasn't for Lady Fate's intervention, we would've been lost to each other that night."

"Well, then it's settled. Carmen listed Julia's cell phone number in the letter. Call her and set up the meeting to take place over dinner tonight."

"You don't mess around, do ya?"

She laughed. "Not when it comes to our happiness. You cared for Julia once, Jake. It won't hurt to see if we can help her now."

He pulled her close and kissed her deeply, thoroughly enjoying the slipping and sliding of her tongue over his. Too bad the flight to Las Vegas was only an hour long. The things he would love to do to her in the bedroom at the back of the plane flew through his mind. Those were going to have to wait until they were alone in their suite at the MGM Grand. "You are one hell of an amazing woman. I love you."

"I love you, too." She lowered her head to whisper in his ear, "Don't think I don't know what's going on in your head, Mr. Hartley. Getting naked with you in that bedroom will have to wait for another trip to Michigan. That particular flight is over five hours long!"

CHAPTER 2

Thirteen Years Ago

High definition television screens covered the entire far wall of the mountainside chalet. Modern technology fascinated The Three. They kept track of their human creations using the very gadgets invented by them. Lucius, in particular, was fond of the wireless technology used in cell phones and personal computers. With a few swift clicks on the keyboard of his laptop, all the screens came to life with pictures of the people they were gathered to discuss. Of course, the gods didn't need the technology to monitor the comings and goings of the humans but they enjoyed passing the time in this manner.

Yeshua, the eldest of the Eternal Siblings, sat in a large, overstuffed easy chair taking in all the lives playing out on the screens before him. His eyes scanned through everything in seconds, immediately recognizing the group as the favorites of his sister, Fate. Once again, she wished to plead their case and asked to be allowed to intervene to make sure their promised destinies would be fulfilled this lifetime. He had refused to let her do more than gently suggest options. Very rarely had he allowed her to step in and directly guide the humans. This time, however, their younger brother sided with Fate. "Lucius, I'm surprised you agree with our sister. You've been very active with this group lately, especially Quinn and Jacob. Why the change of heart? Doesn't it amuse you to see them fail your tests?"

The tall, dark, brooding God of Trials and Tribulations rolled his eyes. "Must you always think so poorly of me? It's not my fault these two haven't chosen the correct paths that would keep them together, Yeshua. You create them. I test them, and Fate guides their destinies. Isn't that what we agreed upon in the Beginning?"

Yeshua chuckled and held his brother's gaze. His normal calm and serene facial expressions had always been enough to keep his siblings in the dark as to what he thought until he chose to fill them in. Tonight, however, he couldn't stop the smile from forming on his lips. For once The Three were in agreement. "It is what we agreed to, but you still haven't answered my questions. What is it about them?" Yeshua pointed at the screens frozen on Quinn's and Jacob's images. "Why are so many other destinies at risk because of *their* poor choices? Why not let them continue on until they finally get it right?"

The second eldest of The Three sighed. She had fought with both of them for so long about their creations, she wasn't sure where to begin. "Through every life, Jacob and Quinn keep choosing paths leading away from each other. Their hearts are always restless because of this, calling out to each other and to me. Right now, Quinn is consumed with the loss of her brother and Jacob's heart is broken, ready to give up on life altogether. If we don't intervene and allow them to finally be together, the lives of the people on the screens before us will be altered forever."

Yeshua raised his eyebrows. "Really? Forever? Aren't you being melodramatic, dear sister? What about all of the others not before us now? Jacob and Quinn aren't tied to any of them, just this small group. In the grand scheme of life, they are but grains of sand. I haven't seen either one of you become so involved with any other humans and certainly not anything else we've created. We have rules for a reason, and each of us has our role to play. Lessons can only be learned if and when life paths are crossed. If they fail, they will have to try again in the next life cycle. Should we make an exception simply because your heart feels sorry for them, Fate?"

Lucius raised his hands. "This is one time I agree with her, Brother. There's little more I can throw at them this time around to test their mettle, but if they keep choosing alternate life paths, my tests will continue. I don't receive pleasure out of their failures, you know. My job would be much easier if they'd simply choose the right path in the first place."

Yeshua smiled again. "You concede there are some humans who are worthy of the blessings we bestow upon them?"

"Don't get too excited, but yes. These two have been pushed to nearly breaking and have somehow managed to keep going lifetime after lifetime. I think with just a few more twists here and there—"

Fate's face reddened. "Lucius!"

"Only to ensure the paths of the other humans involved with them of course." Lucius blew a kiss toward Fate.

Yeshua laughed outright. "Of course." He nodded to Lucius to continue.

"After the little tests, they will be ready. Their destinies are interwoven with so many. You see them as specks of sand, but I see them as making up the beaches of our Island."

Yeshua nodded. He liked where Lucius was going with the analogy. If showed his youngest sibling genuinely cared for humans more than he let on.

Lucius raised a remote control and froze the action on the first screen. "Derek will not find his heart's desire without Quinn entering into his life." The second screen switched to another still picture. "Eric and Jillian won't meet and fall in love as their destinies have foretold without both Jacob and Quinn encouraging them to do so."

The next three screens froze on the face of one man, Steve Eischer. "He will continue to bury himself in his work and lose his chance to find the family he has never had." As each screen froze in place on the face of another of the group, Lucius reviewed the destinies foretold for each of them. "And then there's that sprite, Brigid." Lucius smiled as her face came up on the last two screens. "I have to say she's my favorite. Maybe it's those silver eyes of hers."

Yeshua chuckled and winked. "There's no denying it. You've always been partial to the free spirits, Lucius. Very well. Both of you have convinced me."

The Goddess Fate stood from her chair. "Does this mean I can call in the Guardians?"

The Creator nodded. "Gather them up, Sister."

"Yes, call in your best. You're going to need them."

Lady Fate glared at her younger brother. "Why must you be this way always?"

"Enough." Yeshua cut them both off. "As was said before, this is what we agreed to from the start. The trials Lucius puts before them test their free will. If they hold true even during times of strife, then we shall know they're worthy."

Lucius nodded. "They still must choose the path that leads them to each other, but I won't oppose it. You have my word."

Fate smiled. "Thank you. That's all I ask."

"Who do you choose to help you this time around?" Lucius cleared half of the screens and waited for her answer.

Her emerald eyes twinkled. "Two of our youngest Guardians, Daniel and Michael."

Both of her brothers nodded. Yeshua, in particular, was very pleased with her choices. "Very well. Let's see how it all plays out, shall we?"

CHAPTER 3

Eric ran down the hallway of the hospital's intensive care unit toward the room the nurses had directed him to. He stopped and tamped down the fear that threatened to overtake him. From the moment the call came from his sister Maredyth, his nerves had been raw and his mind dwelled on the absolute worst-case scenario. He had to pull himself together before he saw his mother and sister. He needed to be strong now for them even though he was anything but inside.

Please, let this be a huge mistake. Jake can't be the one here. It has to be someone else.

His silent prayer did very little to ease his anxiety. Eric's stomach churned, and he struggled to keep down what little food he had eaten before he boarded the plane in Las Vegas. He had never seen his brother appear so small or helpless. The tears stung his eyes and blurred his vision, by sheer will alone, he held them back. It took several moments to comprehend the scene playing out in front of his eyes. The patient lying in the bed before him could've just as easily been a complete stranger, except for the long, light-brown hair. Eric would know that unruly mop anywhere. He stood frozen near the door, staring at the battered and broken body of his brother.

Jacob Hartley had been wrapped head to toe in bandages, tubes, and wires. Machines surrounded the head of the hospital bed, whirling and beeping, keeping time with his breathing and heartbeat. His face appeared barely recognizable, colored in various shades of black, blue, and purple. Severely swollen lids hid his eyes from view. Every now and then the respirator took over his breathing, to give his body a moment of rest.

Oh my God! This can't be happening.

Eric approached the bed as his sister reached out for him. They clung to each other. Her body trembled against his, her fear palpable. He lost his composure and gave up all attempts to be strong for his family.

He glanced around the room for his mother, Katrina. She smiled as she stood up from the chair that had been placed close to the bed. She was small in stature, but she appeared to Eric to grow ten feet tall as she walked toward Jacob.

Katrina leaned over, kissed the one part of his stubbly chin not bandaged, and spoke softly near his ear. "Your whole family is here now, Jacob. I'm here, my son. Momma's here. If you can't come back to me, it's okay. Your poppa is there with you, and he will show you the way."

"Mom—Jake's not going to die! It's not his time to go yet." Maredyth's red-rimmed eyes flashed with determination. She reached for one of Jacob's bandaged hands and clutched it tightly.

Eric knew he should try to hide his feelings from his sister, but he struggled, really struggled to find even a spark of hope their brother would ever pull out of this. "Mare—"

"No! We can't lose him, too. Pop has been gone a year—one year! Are you telling me God decided on a whim to take Jake away almost to the very day we lost our father?"

* * * *

"I'm right here, my little girl. I won't ever leave you. Jake needs all of us now. We have to convince your brother to fight his way back." Michael Hartley approached the bed and looked down at his eldest son and middle child. "What were you thinking driving your bike at night during a storm, Jakey?"

"He wasn't thinking clearly, Sarge."

Michael glanced up at the blond, heavily tattooed, and pierced young man leaning against the wall near the foot of the hospital bed. Michael chuckled softly to himself. "You remind me a lot of him you know, full of piss and vinegar. It looks like we've got a lot of work ahead of us here, Danny. Thank you for staying with him after the accident

"I know you did. I expected nothing less than if I had been allowed to be there with you. It's just hard to see one of my children in this state and not be able to fix it like I could when he was little."

The younger angel smiled. "Don't worry. We have a lot of ground to cover with him, and I'm sure there will be plenty of opportunities for you to work your magic. If Fate didn't think we could handle it, she wouldn't have entrusted Jake and the others to our care. She doesn't do that on a whim. Speaking of the others, I just checked in on Quinn. She has thrown herself into her work again and barely hanging on. I left this world not even a month ago, and she's not allowed herself to grieve for me." Daniel peered down at the very battered and broken man in the bed. "Your Jake's our priority this visit. Once we get him to the Island, we can work on getting my sister there, too."

Michael reached out and folded his arms around his wife. Katrina looked as beautiful to him as she did on the day they first met. He wished he could really hold her now, so she could physically lean on him during this horrible time with their son.

Katrina took a deep breath and smiled. Michael knew she felt his presence with them, as always. "Your poppa's here with us, Maredyth."

Eric and Maredyth looked at each other and then back to Katrina with their eyes wide. Eric placed his arm around his sister before addressing his mother. "I sure hope so, Ma. All of us could use him right about now." Maredyth buried her face into Eric's shoulder and cried.

Daniel added his own angelic light and love to that already surrounding the Hartley family. "I bet the two of you visited each other's dreams while you were alive, too."

The elder angel sighed, and his eyes filled with tears. He kept his arms around his wife of over forty years and nodded. "Now and forever. I promised her I would never leave her, no matter what. Not even death can keep me from her and our children."

"It's okay to be scared that your son has lost his way."

"Jake has always been the free spirit of the family. I never worried he wouldn't discover his path eventually. But now?" Michael shrugged and shook his head. "How did my son's life get so out of control so fast?"

* * * *

"How many times do we have to keep discussing this, Jacob? I need you here in LA *with* me, not in some ass-backward farming town back east." Julia Santos piled her raven-black hair on top of her head in yet another style, her hazel eyes blazing at Jacob's reflection behind hers in the dressing-table mirror. "Your mother will have other birthdays. I'll only have one gallery opening, and I need you by my side." A few wisps of hair wouldn't do as Julia commanded, sending her completely over the edge. She slammed her fist into the mirror, shattering it into several pieces. One jagged-edged shard embedded itself in her forearm.

Jacob rushed forward and pulled her away from the rest of the glass. "Hold still! Let me take a look at it. Don't you know you're not supposed to just pull—"

Julia wrapped the fingers of her left hand around the sharp bit of mirror and yanked it out of her arm, slashing her wrist with it. Blood quickly oozed and then suddenly gushed from the wound in spurts.

"Jesus Christ, Julia! What the hell are you doing?" He grabbed her robe from the back of the dressing-table chair and quickly bound her arm tight with it. He made her sit on the bed, away from the rest of the broken mirror and pulled his cell phone out of his pocket. Grateful his EMT training had become second nature for him, he worked quickly and efficiently to finish binding her wounds. He wasn't looking forward to spending another night in the emergency room or having to explain to the doctors how his girlfriend had managed to injure herself again.

She held her arm close to her chest and rocked back and forth. Jacob worried she was heading toward a nervous breakdown. It was her nature to be a bit over the top, but tonight her behavior had been erratic even for her. She grabbed his arm with her free hand and dug her nails into his flesh. "Baby, please don't leave me! Can't you see I'm a wreck without you? Just the thought of you not being here for my—our—grand opening party has my stomach in knots. I can't do it without you. You're my muse. Without you, none of this would be possible. What would people think if you weren't there?" Large tears rolled down her rosy cheeks. Her eyes appeared wild with fright.

Jacob wondered what the hell she could be afraid of now. Was it really the idea of him leaving or just that he wouldn't be there for her twenty-four-seven? He had heard it all many times before. Each time he swore he wasn't going to fall for it again, but his heart just wouldn't let him turn his back on her. Worry she would really go over the edge if he left her now kept him in Los Angeles. The thought she might hurt someone else in the process absolutely terrified him. He hoped his mother would understand. Julia needed him.

God help me. I need her, too. He helped her finish dressing, and together they headed down to the lobby of their building. If luck was on his side, the doorman would already have a cab waiting to take them to the hospital. They had been there so many times over the last six months alone that he was surprised a new hospital wing hadn't been named in her honor.

* * * *

Her admission to the hospital proceeded without incident. No one batted an eye at her explanation as to how she cut her arm. She actually told the truth and basked in all the fuss and fanfare she received from the staff and others in the waiting room. For Julia, being a local celebrity had its perks, and she made damn sure she collected each and every one of them.

All of it took a toll on Jacob, leaving him mentally and physically exhausted. He agreed to leave Julia in the hospital overnight to rest. He needed a break from the chaos that had surrounded their lives as of late. For once she didn't argue with him or insisted he stay with her in her hospital room.

He kissed her forehead as he got up to leave. She murmured softly, and her eyes fluttered a bit but didn't open. He wasn't sure if she was really asleep or just didn't want him to see her without her colored contacts. He had been with her for the last two years and had seen her with every eye color imaginable but still had yet to see her natural color. He had stopped asking about her eye color or anything else for that matter. Julia had always been selective with the personal information she shared with anyone, even with him.

That had been the one area in their relationship Jacob didn't understand. Right from the beginning, he had shared everything with her, not that she had ever been interested in much other than their life together. As she'd told him on numerous occasions, their lives before they met meant nothing. She desired to live in the moment and to hell with the consequences.

He stopped at the nurse's station to make sure they had his new cell number and recognized the woman just reporting for her shift. She smiled brightly when he caught her eye but then frowned, her eyebrows knitted with worry. She moved gracefully through the throng of people gathering near the information desk for the ER to stand next to him as he finished with the ward nurse.

"Mr. Hartley? Are you okay? Is it Ms. Santos again?"

His eyes darted to her name badge. The nurse had been on duty nearly every time he brought Julia into the ER. He tried to smile to reassure her he was doing as well as could be expected, but he was just too beat "Kathy, we have to stop meeting like this."

She smiled and shook the hand he held out to her. "I'm afraid this is about the only place you would be able to find me these days. Since you're not in one of the rooms, I'm assuming Ms. Santos will be staying with us again?"

"The doctor gave her some sort of sedative so she can rest tonight. I'm going to go home and try to do the same. I'll be back to get her in the morning."

The dark-auburn-haired nurse nodded and agreed to call him if there were any problems. "You make sure you get some sleep, too. You'll do no one any good if you stay up all night worrying." She looked him up and down with a critical eye. "You need to take better care of yourself. You look like you've been run over by a semi."

Jacob laughed for the first time that night. "You know, I feel like it. I don't know if I can take much more of this." Jacob didn't know why he said that to this woman who was practically a stranger, but it felt good to get it out in the open.

"Have you looked into getting Ms. Santos some professional help?" Kathy's brown eyes were filled with genuine concern. Jacob wasn't sure if it was for Julia or for him, but at the moment it really didn't matter. He felt relieved that someone else cared enough to come up with the idea.

"Funny you should ask. I brought it up to Julia last week."

"Just before—"

"Just before her last meltdown, yes. Until she agrees to commit herself for treatment, there's little more I can do for her. I can say she tried to kill herself tonight, but I can't prove it. She'll just put on the charm and chalk it up to being exhausted from planning the perfect gallery opening. I don't know what she's so worried about. She's had everything in place for months now, but still, she finds something else to fret over. This time we were arguing while she was doing her hair. It wouldn't go into the style she wanted, so she used the mirror as a punching bag."

Kathy smiled and patted his hand gently. "Don't worry, Mr. Hartley. I'm sure Dr. Carlos will get through to her. He has a wonderful bedside manner, and I'm sure he can convince her to get some help dealing with her emotional issues. Now go on home. Ms. Santos is in good hands."

* * * *

"Quinn, your dedication and work ethic are exactly what we're looking for in a partner for this practice. What's holding you back?" Marshall Hughes was concerned for his best and brightest surgeon. After the death of her brother, he had expected to see her go through a period of mourning and had been prepared to give her however long she needed to regroup.

However, instead of slowing down, she had doubled her caseload, picked up extra shifts, and had amazed everyone with her stamina. That had clinched it for him and had convinced the other partners Quinn was the perfect choice. "You're the kind of leader we want and need to help mentor the staff, especially in light of what we have planned for the emergency hospital."

She smiled. "We've gone through a lot of changes over the last eight years. I have to tell you, what you've planned for the new surgical suites is, well, amazing. Unfortunately, my answer for you is still no. I'm not ready for that step yet."

Marshall shook his head and crossed his arms over his chest as he sat back in the booth "You know, I didn't take your refusal two weeks ago as a firm no, and I just can't do it now either. I'm offering you a chance to make a name for yourself not only as a surgeon but as a world-class instructor. You have the talent and skills to back it up. Why not share it with others? Besides, the emergency staff and our clients adore you. Frankly, you're the best damn surgeon we've ever had."

Quinn laughed hard and waved him off. "Dr. Hughes, please! Your opinion means a great deal to me, but I've had to rethink my goals lately. Things I used to feel were top priorities in my life and my career all suddenly seem so, I don't know, trivial."

He sighed and reached across the table to pat her hand. "With all the hours you've put in here, I'm surprised you've had time to sleep, let alone think about anything else."

She toyed with the food on her plate. "That's true. I've kept myself busy on purpose, hoping an answer would come to me. As much as I love it here, I don't think a partnership is right for me now. Maybe I will feel differently down the road, but for now, I won't be able to give all my attention to it and keep up with the demands of my surgery schedule."

Marshall had thought taking her to one of her favorite spots for lunch would get her to open up and tell him what held her back from joining their partnership. *Maybe it's just too soon after her brother's accident?*

"Do you need time off? You haven't had a real vacation in quite some time. A couple weeks just to yourself may help you figure out what you want from your career. I hope whatever you decide, you make sure it's what *you* want and will make you happy. If there's anything any of us can do for you, you know all you have to do is ask."

She shrugged her shoulders and chewed on her lower lip as she continued to push her untouched meatloaf around her plate. "I would like to take the next month off if that's possible. It's why I've been working like a fiend now. I don't want to leave any of my clients hanging or leave the hospital short staffed."

Relieved to hear her request for time off, he jumped to put her mind at ease and approve her request. Of course, he hoped she would reconsider the partnership, but at the same time, he supported her decision. "Don't you worry about a single thing. You take a month and relax, visit your family, whatever it takes. If you need a longer sabbatical, say the word. You're very important to all of us here as a colleague and a friend."

Her eyes glistened. She grabbed her water glass and drank down half of it. "Thank you. You all mean the world to me, too. I've learned a great deal from everyone, and I appreciate all you've done for me."

Marshall decided not to push her any further. He recognized himself in her eyes. He too had lost a brother. The two of them had many plans of running the emergency hospital and specialty center together. When he died, Marshall lost a part of himself, too, and nearly gave up veterinary medicine altogether. Luckily, he had his family's support, and he had been able to move on. He hoped Quinn found her way sooner rather than later. He hated to think a talent such as hers would be lost because of her personal tragedy.

CHAPTER 4

February 12, Present Day

Quinn stood outside the nightclub at the MGM Grand. During the last three years, she had created many happy memories in the resort. Two years ago, the entire place was renovated using an "angels and fallen angels" theme. Saints and Sinners was the pride and joy of her friend Steve Eischer. Now the mogul used the club to display the art of Quinn's adopted brother.

When Quinn first met Derek a few months after Danny's death, she had been struck by how much he reminded her of her youngest sibling. His love of music, tattoos, and everything to do with the art world had given her such comfort. The immediate bond that had formed between them had been a welcome surprise. For the first time since Daniel's passing, she had enjoyed music again. This change in Quinn had not been lost on her family.

Her parents joined her in Las Vegas the following year to meet him for themselves. From the moment they walked into his fledgling tattoo shop, they had been smitten. A year after their first meeting and several family functions later, Derek had been officially adopted and had changed his last name from Evans to Quartermarsh to honor his new family.

One of the largest paintings he'd ever done was currently showcased at the entrance of the club. The painting had been of Quinn portrayed as a fallen angel with her halo slightly askew and wearing a hot-red minidress. She smiled remembering the very first night she wore the same dress. It had been the night her life changed forever. "Here's where it all started."

"And where I nearly lost you forever." Jacob came up behind her and wrapped his arms around her.

"That was never an option, honey. My heart belonged to you right from the start."

"As mine belonged to you. So much has happened between then and now. It's a wonder we found our way back to each other."

"Well, you did have a little bit of help."

Both of them spun around at the sound of the familiar deep voice behind them. Steve Eischer leaned against a row of slot machines with a sly grin on his face. Quinn smiled and shook her head at him. "Just how long have you been standing there?"

Steve bent down to catch Quinn as she launched into his arms. He swung her around and placed her back on her feet. "I've been pacing around the casino all morning waiting for the two of you to show up." He shook Jacob's hand and then pulled him into a hug as well. "It's been two years since both of you were here, and I want to throw a big Valentine's Day bash to celebrate."

"You don't need to do that. We had hoped to have a low-key visit with you and the gang before the veterinary conference starts up next week." She noticed the look pass between her husband and one of their best friends. She tilted her head and put her hands on her hips. "What have the two of you been up to?"

Jacob glanced over Quinn's head and chuckled. "I told you we couldn't keep this from her for very long."

"Oh, it's not that bad. She didn't cross her arms over her chest or stick her hip out. We're not in too much trouble yet." Steve winked.

"One of you had better start explaining."

"Jake and I have been planning this surprise for you for the last few months. The day after tomorrow this place will be filled to capacity with all of our friends and family celebrating the holiday and your return to Vegas. Enjoy the current decor now, darlin'. Next month Saints and Sinners will get another makeover."

"But I thought you and your partners loved this layout. Why would you change it?" A little pang of sadness formed in the pit of her stomach, but it quickly vanished when she noticed Steve's excited expression.

"Eric and I have been sorting through different ideas. We finally settled on changing up the color scheme a bit but still keeping the 'naughty and nice angels' decor. I've got an interview with an artist from California in a few hours. She's known for her erotic sculptures and paintings. I'm leaning more toward the naughty side of things if you haven't already guessed."

"That artist wouldn't be Julia Santos, would it?" Quinn wrapped her arm around Jacob's waist and hugged him tightly. This was just one more sign they had to meet with her now while she was in Vegas. She thought if Steve was also nearby, Jacob would feel a bit more at ease meeting his old flame.

Steve nodded. "Eric wasn't too keen on the idea, but he refused to tell me why. You care to fill me in? From your brother's reaction to her name, I got the distinct impression his reluctance to speak with Ms. Santos has something to do with you."

Jacob sighed. "It's a long story and one I thought I had left in the past."

"I've learned over the years that it's best just to meet everything head on and let the chips fall as they may. I know as well as anyone the past doesn't always get to stay buried." Steve led them further into the nightclub and back to his office. "I take it this is the first time you've been in contact with her since your accident?"

She should've known. There wasn't much Steve didn't know about any of them. He didn't get to be one of the wealthiest people in the world without keeping tabs on everyone in his life She was grateful he wasn't one of those people who would use the information he had against anyone, that is unless they crossed him or one of his loved ones.

Jacob flopped down on the love seat across from Steve's desk. "It's been nearly thirteen years since we spoke last, and it wasn't very pretty. Now after all this time, I get a letter from her partner asking that I think about meeting with Julia as part of her ongoing therapy."

Steve leaned back against his desk and crossed his arms over his chest. "Are both of you ready for that? I mean, seeing her again could bring up a lot of issues you had with not only her but other women who were in your life afterward. It could rehash the mess the two of you had to wade through to finally be together."

"I'm not afraid of that stuff." she waved her hand dismissively and curled up next to Jacob. "We've been through hell and back to be together, and there's no way giving up a few hours tonight to hear her out will change the way I feel about my husband. I'm not a saint either, as you know."

Steve chuckled. "That I do. So how about you let me spoil Steph and Dan while you're out tonight? Lord knows I'm not going to get much one-on-one time with them after the rest of the family gets into town."

She took Jacob's hand and squeezed. "Didn't I tell you he would be happy to keep the munchkins occupied?"

He leaned over and kissed her. "I never doubted that part of the plan for a minute. I guess I'm not ready to see Julia in person just yet."

"Why don't you tell me what happened leading up to your accident? I know the bare facts of course." Steve smiled and shrugged before plopping down in the leather chair behind his desk. He reached into one of the lower drawers, pulling out a flask of whiskey and two glasses. "I've found that a little liquid courage can go a long way when talking about something painful. Having a somewhat impartial person listen to your story can be very therapeutic."

She rolled her eyes. "Oh, please."

He chuckled again and handed over one of the quarter-filled glasses to Jacob. "Don't give me that look, darlin'. I didn't forget about you. There is a half-dozen bottles of that fruity iced tea you love so much in the minibar next to you."

She grinned and leaned over the cushions to reach the side table that housed the hidden fridge. She selected one of her favorites and nestled back against her husband. "Watch yourself, Mr. Eischer. This time next year, the twins won't be breast-feeding and I'll be back to drinking both of you under the table!"

Both men laughed and tapped their glasses to her bottle. Jacob took a deep breath and let it out slowly as the three of them settled back in their seats. "There are parts of those years with Julia that are still fuzzy, but after the letter arrived the other day, more of the gaps have filled in."

CHAPTER 5

Thirteen Years Ago

Jacob positioned himself at the main bar to get the best view of the guests and observe Julia in her element. Her artwork reflected her personality to a T—attention grabbing and full of heat. Her sculptures were beyond what most would call sensual. Some had actually labeled them borderline pornographic. Anyone off the street would be able to recognize she had used herself as one of the models. The details she included, right down to the dagger tattoo on her right hip, left nothing to the imagination.

His shoulder-length hair, tattoos, scars, and even his fully erect cock were now all on display in her sculptures and paintings. Like it or not, Julia had shared their most intimate encounters with the world and brother both of them into the spotlight. Until she met him, it had been over a year since she had created anything new. Now here they were two years later with a gallery full of her work and packed with the other artists, collectors, and critics in the art world of Los Angeles. Every one of their guests wanted a moment of her time, and one, in particular, caught Jacob's attention.

Dr. Mario Carlos had nonchalantly slipped in next to Julia while she held court with a couple interested in the bronze sculpture of two lovers entwined. Jacob kept his eyes on the doctor as more people joined Julia's discussion group. He moved closer and closer to her, while all eyes were on Julia's face as she talked. Mario slipped his arm behind her and rested his hand in the middle of her lower back.

The hair on the back of Jacob's arms stood on end and his mouth went dry.

What the hell?

He grabbed another shot of whiskey from the line of them he had set up on the bar and tossed it back without looking away from Julia and her group.

She continually scanned the crowd and smiled when her eyes locked on Jacob's. Edging away from Dr. Carlos, she beckoned to her assistant to finish with the delivery instructions for the sculpture and turned her attention to another set of prospective buyers. From Jacob's vantage point, Julia's dismissive behavior hadn't gone over well with the doctor. Mario gulped down his drink and signaled to the servers for another. He elbowed his way through the gallery patrons to reposition himself at Julia's side.

Oh, hell no! Who does he think he is?

It wasn't the first time another man had hit on Julia, and it wouldn't be the last. However, there was something about Mario Carlos that rubbed him the wrong way, especially his behavior with Julia in front of the other guests. He had crossed the line and Jacob had seen enough.

He crossed the room as quickly as he could, never taking his eyes off of her. Another smile slowly formed on her full ruby-red lips. His cock stirred at the sight. His mind conjured up all the ways they would feast on each other when they finally had a moment alone. He fought the urge to pull her into his arms and kiss her right there in front of everyone, especially Dr. Carlos. Why should he stoop to their level of mind games? He knew Julia loved him. He didn't need any huge public displays of affection to prove it.

As he approached, it was Julia who wrapped her arms around him first, holding him close. "There you are, Jacob, darling! I was just telling everyone all the fun we had creating the poses for the sculptures. Mario didn't believe we actually did those things depicted in the artwork. He thinks it's all make-believe, a fantasy if you will."

Jacob smiled and took a glass of champagne from the server who had suddenly appeared on his right. "Whether he believes it or not doesn't matter. We know what went into making those sculptures and paintings. Many hours. One on one." He raised the glass and the others in the group followed, except the now-purple-faced doctor. "Here's to Julia for making *my* fantasies come to life every single day. May her art inspire you to fulfill a few spicy ones of your very own."

Julia kissed him softly and raised her glass again. "Here's to the man who's inspired it all and has more than fulfilled *my* fantasies.

Please join me and raise your glasses in honor of my muse and the star of every woman's erotic dreams, Jacob Hartley!" Cheers erupted throughout the gallery.

This had been one of the happiest nights of his life. His career as a model appeared to be on the verge of taking off thanks to Julia. Anyone else would be thrilled but Jacob worried it signaled the beginning of the end of their relationship. As the evening wore on, Jacob found it hard to concentrate on the conversations going on around him. Instead, his mind flipped through all he had been through over the last few years with Julia. She wasn't like anyone he had ever had any kind of relationship with before, and there had been plenty of times he had felt like a fish out of water around her. Over time, he had become comfortable around her artist friends at parties and at the clubs. It had taken Julia months to get him to even try to fit in at first.

He had thought she was way out of his league when he first laid eyes on her and had been scared shitless when she invited him over to her table. The only way he had been able to keep from embarrassing himself had been to decline her invite and keep with his brother and their friends. While he had bound her to be knockout, he hadn't wanted to be one of those fools used by a rich LA woman and tossed aside when the next best thing came around. Jacob had thought it was over when he left the club that night.

Apparently, Julia hadn't accepted his answer and had found out where he had been staying in town. Two nights later, she showed up at his door and offered him a job as a model. To sweeten the deal, she presented herself as a signing bonus. How could he say no?

He was still trying to find his place in the world and didn't know what he wanted to do with his life. His younger brother had his life going in the right direction. Eric had completed his business degree and had gone off to Vegas to work in a new night club that had opened up at the MGM Grand The salary Julia offered Jacob to pose nude for her had been over the top and more than enough to live off of and still build up a nice-sized nest egg. He had accepted the job and agreed to celebrate their agreement over a drink. That one drink turned into several, and before he knew it, Julia was screaming out his name as he took her from behind.

Not only had Julia gone out of her way to seduce him with her body, she had lavished expensive gifts on him almost daily during the first six months they were an item. His favorite being a custom-built motorcycle. That gift was safely parked in its assigned space in the parking garage attached to the building they now called home. The bike had been part of a photo shoot she had set up, draping models in various stages of undress over him and the motorcycle. The touch of her hands on his body when she posed him along with the other models had sent his body into overdrive. He had tried his best to keep his mind occupied with anything other than having beautiful women slip and slide over his naked body, but in the end, hormones won out and so had Julia.

As soon as she completed all the shots she wanted, she had ordered the other women off the set and had locked the door behind them. Bound to the bike by long, thin strips of soft leather, his back arched over the gas tank, Jacob had been helpless and completely at her mercy. In that position, his cock was fully on display and bouncing with the need for relief. Before he uttered a sound, Julia had straddled him and impaled herself on his cock, grinding her pelvis into his as her pussy pulled every last drop of cum from his body.

All their photo shoots began the same way. At least two other female models were hired to join him acting out each and every fantasy Julia wanted to bring to life in either sculpture or on canvas. After a few hours of being teased, spanked, massaged, and kissed all over, Jacob would be more than ready to fuck Julia's brains out. The faster and harder he took her, the more she liked it and the more she wanted. Julia's appetites ranged from simple and sweet to the more sadistic. Each day he modeled for her, he learned new ways to draw out his own sexual appetites as well as satisfy hers. Jacob enjoyed it all with her and didn't want anyone else. For two years, he thought Julia felt the same about him, but her actions over the last few days nagged at the back of his mind. The doubt grew the more he thought about it.

Will I ever truly be enough for her? Can anyone?

CHAPTER 6

"Why are you making this so difficult? My mother made a special trip out here to meet you and to spend the holidays with the family in San Diego. After we lost Pop last year, she promised she wouldn't let another holiday go by without all of us together under one roof to celebrate. I agreed with her then and still do. Besides, it's time you meet them all, don't you think? The gallery can run without you for a few days."

"As much as I would love to spend the next few weeks with you and your family, I just can't get away. The gallery's taking up all of my time right now, and I've picked up several more commissions. Three of those pieces are to be delivered on the first. That won't happen if I leave town with you. I've sacrificed many holidays to get this far. I don't want to do anything to jeopardize the success of the gallery. I thought you understood that and we were on the same page here." She continued to pack her overnight bag as if to say she was done talking, but he wasn't going to take no for an answer this time.

He knew she could postpone her trip to visit with her clients. She already had enough information to complete all of their commissions and then some. Once again, this was just her way of micromanaging every little detail. Her assistant was more than capable of handling any other issues that popped up. All Julia had to do now was create the artwork the customers ordered and enjoy the profits. All of her hard work was finally paying off, and he wanted her to sit back and enjoy it for a change, especially this year.

He stood behind her and wrapped his arms around her waist. "I know better than anyone how much you've put into the gallery. I feel you need to give yourself a break from all the stress. Please. It would mean the world to me if we spent Christmas with my family." He nibbled on her earlobe, eliciting a sigh from her.

She leaned back against his chest, allowing him to pull her away from her packing. His hands cupped her breasts through her formfitting tank top and found her nipples straining against the fabric. "I want all of them to get to know the woman I love, the one I want to spend the rest of my life with."

Julia sighed loudly. "Your brother can't stand me. I'm sure he's filled your mother's head with all sorts of lies, and I've only talked to your sister over the phone. I think she resents the fact you're here with me and not down there helping her and her husband out with their business. I mean really? Can you see yourself running a group of doggy-day-care facilities?"

"They're much more than that. Just because it has nothing to do with your circle of artist friends doesn't mean it's a waste of time."

"That's not what I meant and you know it. I just see better things for you in your future as a model." She sighed again and turned to face him, searching his eyes. "Are you sure it's what you want? Spending the rest of your life with me could end up bringing you more heartache. What if—?" She looked so uncertain and unsure of herself for the first time since he met her.

He cradled her face in both of his hands and kissed her. "What if nothing. I love you. I can't see myself with anyone else but you."

Tears formed in her now-violet eyes. "No one has ever said that to me before and meant it."

"I do. I have right from the start. I need you by my side when I visit with my family. It's going to be so hard to be with them without Pop. I don't think I can get through this without you."

Her hands slid under his arms to hold him tight. "I still feel horrible for not being with you for your father's funeral, but I didn't want to intrude on your family's grief." She put her fingertips on his lips, silencing his words of protest. "I didn't realize how much this all meant to you. I'll have my assistant clear my schedule for the next week. My clients will just have to understand. You've been by my side through all of this, and now it's my turn. My place is with you."

His lips covered hers once again, finding her tongue more than eager to do battle with his. She quickly undid his belt and the zipper of his pants and slid her hands inside to caress his growing erection. He pulled her tank top over her head and tossed it to the floor. He lifted her off her feet and carried her to the bed he made for her as a Christmas present. The king-sized four-poster bed was crafted out of a dark, richly stained oak with red sheer curtains draping over the top. She squealed with delight when she first saw it set up in their bedroom, and now he hoped to have her squealing again.

She slid out of her boy shorts and up to lay on the pillows. She reached for him as he got rid of the rest of his clothes to join her. "Show me how much you love me, baby. Make me feel it."

He slowly worked his way down her body, licking, nibbling, and tasting as he went. Julia cooed and sighed with every touch along the way, offering her body up for his enjoyment, teasing him with it, knowing full well he couldn't resist her for very much longer. His excitement grew with every sound she made. This was the game they played often with each other, but something felt different to him this time. Something about the way she switched from being adamant she couldn't abandon her clients to wanting to be by his side for the difficult family gathering nagged at the back of his mind. Jacob didn't want to analyze anything at that moment except the beautiful, naked woman underneath him. For, now, he pushed those doubting thoughts to the side and continued to make his lover squirm.

* * * *

Jacob's lips sealed over her clit, drawing out a deep guttural moan from Julia. No man could eat her out like him, and tonight he was in rare form. His tongue glided in and out of her folds with deliberate slow motions that made her entire body burn with the need to have him. While he sucked her throbbing, hooded flesh, his fingers filled up her pussy and stretched her anus. "Oh my God, don't stop."

He feathered and teased her hot, wet folds until the comforter beneath them was drenched with her cum. He slid back up her body, slowly snaking his tongue along a burning trail to her tits. Her nipples were so erect they hurt, just the way she liked them. The slightest touch sent her body over the edge, her cunt twitching with the need to be completely filled with his cock. To emphasize that point, she pulled her legs up and wrapped them around his hips. "Fuck me, now, Jake. Let me have that glorious dick of yours deep inside me."

Her breathing quickened as the head of his cock eased into her so slowly. She tried to pull him in fast, but he only smiled and held his position. He tugged her arms up over her head and quickly bound them in the leather straps attached to the headboard. Julia returned the smile. She loved the feel of the strap around her wrists and in her palms. Jacob really did know how to please her, in every way. Having her hands bound while she was willingly ravaged by a man had always been a fantasy of hers, and now she could mark that off of her bucket list.

Julia clenched her fingers tightly around the leather as Jacob shoved her legs further apart and buried his cock in her cunt. The sensation overwhelmed her, and yet her body craved more. He pulled out quickly and sat up, lifting her ass off the bed as he went. Now with half of her body suspended in the air, he entered her again, slowly working her up and down his cock, gradually building up to the speed she craved. Her tits bounced hard with each thrust. Her thighs quaked and were soon slick with her own juices, and yet he still loved her, still took more and more from her. Julia's mind went blank with one final full-body orgasm.

She came to her senses as Jacob released her from the leather straps and pulled her close to curl up to his body, her head resting on his chest. As she listened to his heartbeat slow down to its normal soothing rhythm, she fought to hold back the tears that threatened to fall.

What the hell's wrong with me? Why can't this be enough? Why can't Jacob be enough?

* * * *

The bar was filled to near capacity on a rainy night just three days before Christmas. He really shouldn't be out on a night like this, but after he got the call from an upset Kathy, he had to venture out on his motorcycle in the weather. She had been frantic on the phone, telling him that she had to talk to him before he left town. Kathy had been nothing but kind and caring at the hospital and always took great care of Julia. He had come to see her as a friend, one of the very few he had in LA. He felt obligated to help her get through whatever was troubling her. Jacob owed her that much. Each visit to the hospital with Julia brought up so many bad memories of his father's illness and death. He never would've made it through any of it if Kathy hadn't been a sympathetic ear. She had helped him realize he wasn't crazy, he was just still grieving for the loss of his father. She had helped him remain calm with each visit to the emergency room.

He found her in a booth near the back, just as she said she would be. She seemed relieved to see him as he slid into the seat across from her. "Thank you for coming here to meet me tonight. With the weather, I thought maybe you would cancel."

"Whatever it is must be damn important. You sounded a bit freaked out on the phone. I didn't think you could tell me everything that was bothering you unless it was face to face."

She took a gulp of her beer and nodded her head. "This is so hard. I've been trying to wrap my mind around the whole thing for days now. I'm not really sure how to begin. It's all a bit surreal. If I wasn't there to see it for myself, I wouldn't have believed it."

His confusion and worry for her mounted. On the phone a half hour ago, she had been in a panic to get him to agree to meet her in person to discuss something, but now she was unsure where to start. "What're you trying to tell me? It sounds like you've witnessed something you shouldn't have?"

Kathy only nodded, took another gulp of her beer, but still held her tongue.

"I'm sure it's really not as bad as you think. Whatever it is, you might as well just tell me and get it out in the open. I'm still not clear as to why you feel you need to tell me about this…whatever it is. But if it makes you feel better talking about it, just put it out there."

"It's about Ms. Santos and Dr. Carlos." Kathy's eyes flew open wide as the words rushed from her mouth in one breath.

The hair on Jacob's arms stood at attention once again at the mention of Julia and Marlo. Those were the last words he thought would come out of Kathy's mouth. His mind reeled with conflicting thoughts of bolting out of there before she said one more thing and shaking her to make her spill everything she knew. Jacob swallowed hard and took a few deep breaths before he found his voice. "What about them?"

"I saw them together. They didn't know I was in the supply room with them."

Jacob clenched his fists. "What do you mean, Kathy? Were they arguing? What?"

Tears rolled down her flushed cheeks. "Not arguing. I'm sorry, Jake, but they were having sex, right there in the supply closet. He had her pinned against the wall—"

"Why are you telling me this?" His thoughts jumbled and his vision blurred a bit. Jacob fought to keep the bile down that churned violently in his stomach before he tried to speak again. He knew it. He knew it all along and he just didn't want to admit it to himself. "Maybe it wasn't them. You could've been mistaken."

"I wish I was." Kathy wiped the tears from her face and took another gulp of her drink. "I finally got up the nerve to confront him about it a few hours ago. I mean, talk about crossing the line with one of your patients! I looked up to him and respected him and his medicine. I couldn't believe he'd be one of those kinds of people."

Jacob struggled to keep calm and listen to everything she was explaining to him. "What did he?"

"He laughed and told me to mind my own fucking business. Mario told me that if I didn't keep my mouth shut, he'd see to it that I no longer had a job…anywhere." Kathy's sobs finally tore through her and she covered her face with her hands. "I'm sorry to tell you this, but I just couldn't keep quiet. I don't care if he does get me fired. I couldn't sit back and watch them hurt you anymore. The two of them have put you through enough."

Jacob's mind flashed on all of the nights spent in the emergency room. Each and every single time, Dr. Mario Carlos was there to help take care of Julia. How could he be so blind? He reached across the table and held Kathy's hands. "I know this was hard but thank you for telling me. I knew something just wasn't right with Julia for a while now, but I never dreamt that she was sleeping with Carlos. I thought he was chasing after her, but never did I think she was actually fucking him."

"I wish I would've figured it out sooner."

He laughed and immediately regretted it. That's when he finally noticed the sad look in her eyes and the way she slumped in the booth. *Oh my God! She's a victim, too.* "You're in love with him, aren't you?"

Kathy nodded. "We've been working together for ten years and seeing each other off and on for the last seven. He has the fucking nerve to tell me to mind my own business? It *is* my business! The last few months he was talking about getting married. He wanted a huge, lavish affair, black-tie and all."

"Sounds like he made a lot of plans for your future together."

She snorted and wiped the tears from her cheeks. "Only problem is I was too stupid to figure out he wasn't talking about marrying me. I don't think he's ever loved me. It has always been Julia Santos. How the hell can I compete with her? Appearance is everything to Mario. Of course, he wants someone as hot as Julia on his arm instead of me. How could I have been so stupid?"

Anger, confusion and hurt consumed. *Why didn't I confront her when I first suspected something wasn't right between us?*

How could Julia just keep going on living with him like nothing was wrong? How many other men had fucked her since they were together? His mind raced through the possibilities, all the times she went out of town on business, refusing to be around when his family came to visit. He hadn't wanted to think about any of it then and sure as hell not now. It hurt just too damn much, and to top it all off, someone else he cared about had been hurt in the process.

He wanted to be numb to it all. He signaled to the waitress before he reached across the table for the half-full beer stein. Jacob closed his eyes and chugged down the last of Kathy's beer in one swallow. "Looks like both of us are going to need another drink."

CHAPTER 7

He wasn't going there to confront her. Really, he wasn't. He planned to grab the bags he had packed earlier and head out early to see his family. He needed to be away from her and think things through. Still, something in the back of his mind told him he wanted to hear it directly out of her mouth. Until that was done, it didn't seem real to him. How could Julia make him give up everything, including time with his family, if she didn't want him around anymore? Was it all some twisted game? Was he just a new toy that she would toss away as soon as something better came along? His mind wouldn't stop with the questions, even after the pitcher of beer he had shared with Kathy over the last several hours. He made sure she was safely in a cab before he finally left the bar and headed back to what he once thought of as home.

The rain was really coming down by the time he pulled his motorcycle into the garage of their building. His teeth chattered and he felt chilled to the bone. Jacob's clothes were drenched and clung to his skin. He was definitely in need of a hot shower before hitting the road again. Maybe he should just spend the night in a hotel and drive in the morning when the weather was better? Anywhere but in their condo would suit him just fine.

The sound of music filled his ears as soon as he opened the door. The lights had been dimmed in the living room, but it wasn't too dark to prevent him from seeing pieces of men's clothing on the floor near the couch. The hallway leading toward the master bedroom was lined with candles and a few more garments he recognized as Julia's lingerie. In fact, they were part of the set he had given to her for her birthday four months ago. His stomach churned with each step he took down the corridor. The bitter taste of his own bile filled his mouth when he finally reached his destination. The door to the bedroom was only open about a foot, but that was all he needed to see and hear, what was going on.

Any thoughts he had entertained that his relationship with Julia would go on completely left his mind the instant he peered into the room. There they were on the bed he made with his own two hands. Julia faced the doorway with her eyes closed and her arms braced behind her on her lover's abs as she plunged up and down on an enormous cock. Neither one of them noticed Jacob standing there in disbelief, dripping rainwater on the thick white carpet.

"Baby, your pussy's all I ever think about. I love the way you ride my cock!"

I know that voice! She's fucking him right here in our bed!

Jacob tried to speak, but the words wouldn't come out. His throat seized up, barely allowing him to breathe. This was one of his worst nightmares come to life. He couldn't move or close his eyes to the scene playing out in front of him.

Julia was another story. Her eyes opened slowly and seemed to take a moment to comprehend he stood there watching them. Instead of stopping, she picked up the pace and smiled broadly. She tossed her head back and shouted over her shoulder, "I love riding your cock, Mario. I can never get enough of it filling me up."

Jacob's body finally responded to the commands from his brain. He crossed the room swiftly and pulled Julia from the bed. Mario bellowed a protest at the sudden motion of her off his dick but froze once he made eye contact with Jacob. "Don't you fucking move, Carlos."

"Let her go, Hartley. It's been over between the two of you for some time now. She doesn't want anything to do with you or your family. Not now. Not ever again."

Jacob turned back toward the still-smiling and obviously drunk Julia. His heart pounded, as he searched her eyes for any hope that this night was all a dream. As ever, her eyes were unreadable through those goddamn contacts. "That true?"

She giggled and then laughed outright. "God, what does it take for you to get the hint? I don't need you anymore. The gallery opening was a success. I'll be busy for the next year creating new pieces from all the commissions generated from the opening."

"That's all I ever was to you? A plaything until your gallery took off?"

"I do have you to thank for that, but eventually I'll need a new muse. It was fun while it lasted, but it's time for you to move on, baby. It's better this way, trust me."

Mario tried to get up from the bed but was still tangled up in the sheets. Jacob saw his chance and swung at him. He forgot he was holding his helmet until the moment it connected with the doctor's jaw, knocking him out cold.

"Get the fuck out of here, Jake!" Julia's eyes flashed angrily as she yanked her arm from his grip and stood her ground. She didn't move a muscle to help her naked and unconscious lover. She cared about one thing and one thing only—herself. Jacob's heart had finally reached its breaking point.

"As always, you get what you want, Julia, and to hell with anyone who gets in your way. This time, you've gone too far. One day you'll find yourself all alone, with no one there to be your muse or your doormat." Jacob stormed out of the condo, barely making it to the elevator before his knees buckled. Somehow, he kept standing the entire ride down to the lower level. Thankful he didn't run into anyone on the way down, Jacob moved swiftly toward his motorcycle to discourage any conversation from those waiting to get on the elevator he was exiting. He didn't want to talk to anyone about anything. He just wanted to get far away as fast as his bike could carry him.

Even with the slick weather conditions, he was on the highway within minutes. There weren't many cars on the road during the downpour, so it was easy for him to zip in and out of traffic even going nearly 95 miles an hour. If he kept up the pace, he would be in San Diego within two hours. Maybe he'd just keep on driving and call his sister from the road when either he or his motorcycle finally ran out of gas.

Jacob became more and more distracted as his mind replayed the scene in the condo. So much so, he never saw the piece of wood in the middle of his lane until he hit it. The last thing he remembered was flying through the air and slamming into the back of a semi.

* * * *

"Oh my God! Keep honking your horn and flashing your lights, Dave. If that truck driver doesn't stop soon, he's going to drag that guy for another three miles." Dave's wife frantically dialed 911 to report the accident. As she spoke to the dispatcher, she glanced around and noticed several other people in the cars traveling close to them on cell phones. She hoped with enough calls, help would somehow arrive faster. The further the truck went along the I-5 the less likely the motorist would survive.

"The dispatcher said to keep doing what you're doing to get that truck to stop, honey. They're sending squad cars to block off the freeway down the line. God help that poor man!"

The sudden flash of the semi's brake lights brought the entire gruesome caravan to a halt. Several people darted out of their cars to rush to Jacob's aid. The driver of the truck came around the back and immediately fell to his knees. "I didn't know! Please let him be okay."

Dave and two other men helped to untangle Jacob's body from the back and undercarriage of the truck. "Be careful, guys. He's gonna be in a whole world of hurt by the looks of things." Once they had him safely away from the semi, Dave quickly assessed the extent of Jacob's injuries and relayed it to his wife, who still was on the line with the police dispatcher. "His pulses are weak but present. Maybe a few broken ribs, but he's breathing okay for now. One of his arms is broken and at least one bone in his leg is shattered and poking through his jeans."

"The dispatcher said to leave his helmet on, honey. The paramedics should be here any minute to finish stabilizing him."

He nodded. "Tell them the helmet is cracked but otherwise still in one piece. That has to be something of a miracle if you ask me."

She relayed the information and was grateful her husband was able to stay so calm. She couldn't stop shaking. She was sure the motorcyclist was dead as soon as his body flew into the back of the truck. The fact he was still alive nearly made her weep. "Someone from heaven must be really looking out for you, young man." As the sound of the sirens grew louder, Dave's wife reached out and held Jacob's bloody hand. "Hold on. More help is on the way."

* * * *

Daniel surrounded Jacob with his angelic light to protect him from any further harm. Normally this type of shielding was a huge drain on his powers, but with the help of the other angels nearby, he was able to keep him safe. He arrived just as Jacob's body hit the back of the truck and was able to block his mind from remembering any more of the accident or the pain. Daniel hadn't been allowed to intervene sooner even after pleading with Lady Fate. Michael hadn't been permitted to be present for any of this, so instead, he was with his family waiting for the news of the accident.

The paramedics and fire department finally arrived on the scene along with several highway patrol cars. As the police officers gathered up the motorists for their statements, the fireman concentrated on Jacob. One of them turned away and vomited after getting one look at his mangled body. "Who helped move him away from the truck?"

Dave stepped forward. "We moved him as carefully as we could. Didn't know if he was breathing or not, so we thought it best to get him to level ground and keep him warm until you all got here."

The gray-haired paramedic nodded. "You did the right thing leaving that helmet of his on, too. We'll keep it on during transport and let the docs cut it off him there. This guy has a chance to make it through this because of your cool head."

Dave blushed. "Nah. It's just my medic training kicking in. If he makes it out of this, it's because he has a few Guardian Angels watching over him. I've never seen someone dragged like that live."

"Honestly, neither have I."

Daniel stood by as they quickly loaded Jacob into the back of the waiting ambulance and sped off down the freeway. Dave was right. Most people wouldn't survive this kind of beating, but Lady Fate and Yeshua had plans for Jacob Hartley, and it was Daniel's job to make sure he made it through. As the sirens blared through the stormy night, the Guardian settled in beside his charge so he could whisper in his ear. "Just rest now, Jake. You're in good hands. You can have a long life ahead of you, but first, you've got some serious soul-searching to do."

CHAPTER 8

February 12, Las Vegas, Present Day

"Will you relax, honey. The maître d' assured us we'll have a quiet table away from the majority of the dinner guests. If you want to have more privacy, we can still have the meeting in the suite and order dinner sent up to us."

Jacob tightened his grip around Quinn's waist, hoping to steady his nerves a bit. When the hostess told them Julia was already seated at the table, he fought the urge to run in the other direction. Now here he was within a few feet of seeing the woman who he at one time thought was his everything.

Here goes nothing.

Julia had been seated so she faced them. She appeared to be perusing a menu as they approached. She looked as elegant as he remembered her. Her once-waist-length raven-colored hair was now styled in an asymmetrical bob that suited her features. She smiled as she stood to greet them. What surprised him the most was Julia genuinely appeared happy and even relieved to see him standing in front of her in the restaurant.

"Thank you both for coming." The three of them stared at each other for a beat or two before Julia giggled softly. "Where are my manners? I'm so glad both of you agreed to meet me here in Vegas. You must be Quinn. The portrait of you in Saints and Sinners really does capture your beauty." She shook first Quinn's hand and then gripped Jacob's firmly with both hands. Jacob was surprised to feel that they were shaking just as badly as his own. "This means a great deal to me you've come. Please, have a seat."

He helped Quinn with her seat and sat down next to her. "I wasn't sure it was a good idea, but my wife convinced me it was time we were face to face again."

Julia's gray eyes glistened with unshed tears. "I agree. It's definitely the right time for us to see each other. I have a confession though. I've been terrified of this moment for the last few years. I know what I did to you was beyond reprehensible."

"Why do you think it's necessary for us to go through all of that pain again? Can't we just let it go and move on? It's worked for me so far."

Quinn gripped his leg under the table. It was their signal to help him remember to calm down.

"Okay, maybe not so good up until a few years ago."

All three of them laughed and appeared to relax a little bit more. The waiter brought over their drinks and a few appetizers. Jacob was thankful for the little distraction but knew it was best to keep things moving along. "I don't mean to belittle your need to make amends, but I'm having a hard time seeing how it can help you."

Julia looked at Quinn. "What about you? How do you feel about meeting me? I'm sure Jake's filled you in on our past together. You must think I'm a Grade-A bitch."

"Honestly, I'm not the best person to judge what you did or didn't do in your past. I do believe everyone deserves a second or even a third chance at happiness. From your girlfriend's letter, it seems you've been working very hard at finding your happily ever after."

"I have. It's taken a lot of years of therapy to go through all the crap in my life to find out why I did the things I did. It all comes down to allowing the walls I put up as a kid to come tumbling down. I finally accepted that there were people in the world who could actually care about me for me and not what they could get out of me. Jake was the one who showed me that."

"Then why did you push me away? I did everything you wanted me to do, and still, it wasn't enough." His chest tightened and his head pounded. The accident flashed through his mind. "Why?" He reached for Quinn's hand under the table and held on for dear life. "Why did you tear my heart out and crush my spirit?"

Julia bit her lower lip and wiped the now-free-flowing tears from her face with her napkin. "Because I could."

CHAPTER 9

Thirteen Years Ago

Kathy sprinted through the hallway toward the nurse's station on the ICU floor. One of her friends was on duty that night and called her as soon as Jacob was transported to the ER. Kathy had just finished a long, hot bubble bath and was heading to bed when the call came in. Dropping her phone to the floor, she made a mad dash back to the bathroom. She barely got the toilet seat up before she vomited.

What the hell have I done?

Jacob was fighting for his life, and he wouldn't be there if it hadn't been for her.

She didn't know what she was going to do once she saw him, but she felt she had to be there for him and his family or at least try to be. Her already-frazzled nerves calmed a bit as she listened to the floor nurses describe Jacob's current condition after surgery. She asked a few more questions before making the trek to his room. Usually, only family members were allowed in, but since she was on staff and a nurse, she hoped they would make an exception for her. If not, then she would at least leave her name and number for the Hartley family and let them decide if they wanted to contact her.

As she approached, a young man in his mid-to-late twenties smiled and walked toward her. He had multiple piercings in both ears and a myriad of visible tattoos. There was a soft glow about him that made her feel at ease instantly. As he moved closer, she was immediately drawn to his eyes, the most amazing blue-green eyes she had ever seen. She couldn't keep from staring into them.

"Can I talk to you a moment, Kathy?" Even the sound of his voice brought her comfort. She didn't understand what was happening, but she wasn't complaining, not one bit.

"How do you know my name?" Her own voice sounded foreign to her. Instead of her usual confident tone, she sounded tentative and shy. *What's wrong with me? He just wants a moment of my time.* She smiled and held her hand out to him. Maybe he was one of the new ICU doctors she heard so much about or even one of the Hartleys?

"It's a long story and one I'll be happy to fill you in on once we have more time. Before you go in there, you have to know you're not responsible for this. You have to believe that with all your heart." A comforting warmth spread through her as he took her hand. "Jake needs all the help he can get to make it through. His family will need someone to help make sense of all the medical jargon. We think you'd be the best for the job."

"I don't understand. Who, what are you?" As soon as the words left her mouth, she knew. "Are you an—"

"An angel? Yep. I know I'm not what you'd expect, but I am."

Kathy's knees finally gave out. She needed to sit down and fast. Daniel helped her to the chair outside of Jacob's room.

"My name's Daniel, but you can call me Danny. You'll be seeing me from time to time, along with my partner, Michael. He's in there now with his family."

She looked through the glass and saw an older man with a faint glow about him, just like Daniel's. Her eyes widened, and she gasped. "Is that Jake's father?"

Daniel nodded. "His place is right there for now. I did what I could to help Jake forget most of the accident, but he has a very long road ahead of him if he's to recover from this. What do you say? Are you in?"

"I'm not sure I'm the best for the job." Fresh tears filled her eyes. "I'm the one who told him about his girlfriend, so he may not want me around. I wouldn't blame his family if they banned me altogether."

"Why would you say that?"

Kathy hung her head in shame. "I was feeling sorry for myself after finding out that the man I was in love with no longer cared for me one bit. Hell, who am I kidding? Mario never cared about me at all, ever." She shrugged her shoulders and raised her eyes to meet

Daniel's. "Maybe I wanted someone else to feel just as badly as I did? God, I wish I would've kept my mouth shut."

"It's only human nature to try to find comfort when your heart is broken. Jake didn't blame you before his accident, so you shouldn't do so now. Trust me. He wants you to be here and so does his family. He put himself in that bed with his reckless driving in this weather. It wasn't what you said that put him in such a state."

"I suppose not. It was my ex and Ms. Santos who've caused so much pain for both of us." Kathy's mind immediately conjured up the image of the two of them going at it in the supply closet. *Oh no!* "Did he see the two of them together after what I told him tonight?"

Daniel shrugged. "What he did or didn't see is beside the point. Don't worry about any of that. Just do what you do best."

She nodded slowly, thinking about all that had happened that day. "I'm back on duty tomorrow afternoon, but I really would like to check in with them, if you're sure they won't mind."

Daniel smiled broadly and made Kathy feel warm all over once again. "I'm sure. Go ahead. They've been expecting you. Dr. Evans spoke very highly of you to the Hartleys. He's in charge of Jake's case and apparently handpicked you to be on his team."

She blushed a little at the compliment. "Dr. Evans is an amazing doctor, and I'm honored he thought of me for Jake's care." Kathy stood up, took a deep breath, and slowly entered the room.

A petite older woman, presumably Jacob's mother Katrina, looked up as she neared the bed. "Are you my son's friend, Nurse Baker?"

"Yes, ma'am. I came as soon as I heard he was here." She looked over at her friend badly bruised and nearly completely covered in bandages and wanted to cry all over again. "I…I'm so sorry."

Maredyth turned and reached for her hand. "Dr. Evans tells us you'll be one of his nurses. Come on in and tell us a bit about yourself. It looks like we're going to be seeing a lot of each other."

Eric pulled another chair close to the bed and offered it to Kathy. "Why don't you sit down? Once my sister starts the twenty questions, you'll be glad you have a comfortable seat."

He winked and smiled the same smile Kathy had seen on Jacob's face many times. Daniel was definitely right. She needed to be there for Jacob and his family. She'd have to use every one of her skills as a nurse to help them all to heal, including herself. When chaos surrounded her, she found peace at the hospital. The only thing that kept her on track was caring for her patients, and now one of her friends was fighting for his life. The least she could do was help care for him while he did it.

* * * *

Michael stood back and watched his family welcome the still-somewhat-shell-shocked Kathy into their ranks. With her there to help explain the medical terms and what to expect with Jacob's tests and treatments, he felt comfortable leaving. It was time he joined Daniel on the Island.

He wished he could've been at the accident site to add his protective healing energy, but the Big Guy forbade it. Michael had to admit he was mad at first, okay, extremely pissed off was more like it, but now he understood the logic. He would've been of no use to his son if he was there. Watching Jacob flying through the traffic on his motorcycle would've been bad enough, but to see him slam into the back of the truck and then be dragged under it was definitely more than Michael would've been able to take.

Walking through the quiet hallway of the ICU, he nodded at several other Guardian Angels on duty. A few of them were watching over their own family members, but most were simply assigned to other wards in need of guidance. Michael was grateful for his assignment, but tonight was the first time in the last year he questioned it. He wasn't sure how he was going to convince his son he needed to fight and come back to this world. Lady Fate had reassured him that Jacob would finally be with his true soul mate. How long they would have together now was something neither he nor Daniel was privy to at the moment.

There were a few other charges he had to check in on before heading for the Island. So many paths were available to each and every one, but it was their own decisions that determined which direction they would go. Daniel and Michael could offer bits of guidance here and there, but they couldn't directly intervene without special permission from Lady Fate. She alone knew how it all would turn out on each path. Sometimes she intervened herself when things weren't going the way she wanted them to proceed. The Island was her way of doing so with Jacob. She was counting on the angels to convince him to fight for his life. By showing him the love that could be his if he only reached out for it, Michael hoped he could give his son the courage to live again.

CHAPTER 10

The waves crashed on the beach, bringing him out of his dream with a start. Jacob bolted straight up out of bed in a panic. "Where the hell am I?" He stared at his reflection in the mirrored walk-in closet. He looked the same, other than the fact he was stark naked and deeply tanned.

"Where the fuck are my clothes?" He glanced around the bungalow, his eyes adjusting to the slightly darkened room. The curtains of the sliding glass doors gently billowed into the room from the balmy sea breeze. He found a pair of jean shorts on the chair near the door and slipped them on. He headed outside to check out his surroundings.

Just outside his quarters, he discovered a large patio, barbecue pit, and bubbling hot tub. By the looks of the vegetation, he thought he could be somewhere in the Pacific Islands, maybe even Hawaii or Tonga. Then again, maybe he was on someone's private island. It really didn't matter. He just wanted to find out what the hell was happening to him. Jacob didn't understand how he was in California one moment and then the next on a tropical island at sunrise.

Two figures walking along the beach appeared in his sight. He waved to them as they moved up the sand toward his bungalow. The younger man looked about his brother Eric's age, covered in tattoos, and something about his eyes made goose bumps pop out all over Jacob's skin. They were blue green like the ocean, and Jacob couldn't make himself stop staring at them until the older man spoke.

"Welcome to the Island, Jakey."

His mind didn't believe what he was seeing. His vision blurred and then cleared the moment his eyes locked with Michael's. Jacob's knees weakened, and the younger guy reached out to steady him.

"Pop? How? Am I dead?"

Michael took Jacob's free arm and helped Daniel escort him back to the patio to sit down. "Not exactly. This is what the Big Guy Upstairs calls Limbo. We like to refer to it as the Island. It has a better ring to it, don't you think?"

"This is definitely not like what I thought Limbo was supposed to look like. I don't understand how I got here. One minute I'm packing my bag to visit Maredyth for Christmas, and the next I wake up here naked in a strange bed."

"That would be my doing. You were in a bad accident with your bike, brotha."

"Did I hurt anyone else?" The panic rose inside him, threatening to take over. "What happened to Julia? Was she with me on the bike?"

Michael sighed. "Let him see a bit, Danny. If you don't, he won't believe anything we have to tell him."

Daniel frowned. "Okay, but don't say I didn't warn you." He closed his eyes, and a white glow surrounded the three of them. All could see what happened a few hours ago as if they were there witnessing it again first hand.

Jacob's head exploded with the lightning flash of images zipping through his mind. Each scene played out in front of them on fast-forward. The conversation with Kathy at the bar flew by his eyes, followed swiftly by the fight with Julia and Dr. Carlos in the condo. Lightning flashed, and he felt the wind in his face as if he was riding his Harley again. The last he remembered was the highway wet with the Christmas rain, and then the semi was suddenly in his path. The impact of his bike against the wood in the road jarred his teeth, and then he was flying through the air. He put his head in his hands and groaned. "I don't want to remember anymore."

"Here, let me help you." Daniel placed one hand over Jacob's eyes and the other cradled the back of his head. A gentle heat washed over them both and the pain faded away.

"How'd you do that?" Jacob rolled his shoulders and ran his fingers through his hair. His hands were still shaking a little after reliving what led up to his accident. He clenched his fists and held them tightly against his legs, hoping to calm down the rest of the way.

Daniel smiled. "It's a trick of the trade. Something we hope you won't learn for many more years to come."

Michael reached for Jacob's hands. "I know this is all overwhelming for you, but we need your full attention now." Jacob nodded for his father to continue. "You were brought here for a reason. It's not your time yet, but you have to want to go back and live, Jakey."

"What happens if I decide not to go back?"

His father's face fell and tears rolled down his bearded chin. "There's nothing written that says you have to go back. It's your choice, but it's imperative you understand this. If you stay, you *will* miss your chance to be with your always and forever. You won't get the joy of holding your children for the very first time, and you'll never know the love of a beautiful woman who needs you as much as you need her, heart and soul."

Jacob shook his head sadly. "That's not ever going to happen for me, Pop. I thought I had it with Julia, and she played me for the fool that I am. It happened for Mare and I'm sure it will happen for Eric someday, but not for me. I'm tired of searching for what will never be. I'll never find someone to love and who loves me like you loved Ma. What you had together was once in a lifetime. I don't deserve that kind of happiness."

Daniel stared at him with his eyes wide. "So, you mean to tell me you just want to give up? We're offering you a chance to experience the kind of love your parents had and still have. It's a blessing from Lady Fate herself."

"Why waste your time? It's just going to fall apart anyway. Everything I touch tends to do that. No matter what I do, I can't seem to get ahead. I always end up back home with my parents. Some catch I'll be for anyone. Probably best if Fate blessed someone else more deserving."

Daniel's bawdy laugh caught Jacob off guard. "Yep. You were right, Sarge. He's stubborn as a mule. Quinn will definitely give him a run for his money!"

Jacob's confusion grew. Not only was he on some tropical island with two angels, he was supposed to meet someone else. "Who's Quinn?"

"She's my sister and *your* destiny. She'll be here soon and you'll see for yourself."

"Quinn is in Limbo, too?"

"Not exactly. She's learning to come here to escape in her mind, through her dreams. She can decompress here and just let go. Quinn's going through hell now. I died almost a month ago on Thanksgiving. She hasn't really dealt with it very well at all." Daniel's eyes clouded over at the mention of his sister's grief. He cleared his throat and smiled again. "We're here now to change all of that. Right here on the Island, you'll get to meet and fall in love with the one who completes your heart and soul."

Jacob groaned. "So, what are you? Cupids for God?"

Daniel's laugh boomed out over the patio again. The sound was infectious, and this time Jacob laughed along with him. "You could say that. From what I know about my sister, you're exactly her type, and both of us would approve of your ink, brotha!" Daniel glanced behind Jacob and noted the empty space on the skin of his back. "But I do think you need a few more. How would you like a couple dueling dragons covering your back?"

"Hey now, Danny! Don't go covering him up with tattoos before Quinn gets to meet him." Michael leaned over and looked at Jacob's back and nodded. "I agree with you though. He could use a bit of color, at least on his shoulders. From what you told me, I think your sister would agree with the dragon choice. She might even want to see you get them. Of course, that's once she conquers her fear of needles."

"Give me a little more time, a few more nudges, and my sister will be sitting in a tattoo artist's chair soon enough. Once you get one, you have to get another. It's just the way it is."

Michael turned back to his son. "The only ones I have on my body were from my time in the Corps. Don't tell your mother, but when you came home with your first tat, I really wasn't mad you went behind my back to get it."

Jacob laughed. "Well, it would have been nice if you let me in on that. The whole neighborhood heard you bellow at me that day."

"Well, I was mad you didn't ask me to go with you."

Daniel and Jacob both did double takes before all three of them cracked up once again.

"What? Do you think you kids have the corner on the tattoo market? I appreciate good ink when I see it and can definitely appreciate a beautiful woman. You wait until you meet Quinn. She'll take your breath away, just like your mother did to me the very first day I laid eyes on her."

CHAPTER 11

The tears rolled freely down her cheeks as she turned the pages of the photo album filled with pictures of her brother, Daniel. The emptiness in her heart consumed her. She didn't understand why he had to be struck down so young. He had everything ahead of him. His band pulled in large crowds in the local bars in Detroit and had several concert promoters competing for the chance to have them open for the big-name groups touring through Michigan. Another passion of his had been tattoo art. Daniel had taught himself how to use the equipment and basically made a pest of himself until his favorite tattoo artists took him under their wings and helped him hone his craft. He had quite a large following of regulars clamoring to have him put his creations on their bodies. Their sister Miranda's three small boys considered him the best uncle on the planet. Not a day went by Daniel wasn't dragging at least one of them around the house. Usually, all three would tackle him at once, but the end result was always the same. Their laughter still rang in her ears and tugged at her heart.

The last picture in the album was of the two of them visiting the coolest shop near Frankenmuth. It was filled with everything metaphysical, from candles to rune stones to fairies and her favorite, dragons. They were on a mission at the shop to find a book their cousin Brigid recommended. Together, with the aid of the book, they were going to teach Quinn how to dream walk. Both Brigid and Daniel filled her head with their stories of being able to do it, and Quinn wanted to see if she could experience it as well. Her scientific mind told her it wasn't possible, but she tried to keep an open mind and wanted to give it a try herself.

Quinn slid the album back into its spot on the top shelf of the bookcase Daniel had made for her. Besides the photo albums, the shelves were filled with books about Wicca, angels, dragons, and other fantastical creatures. She shared the love of these things with her brother and cousins, but now she couldn't bring herself to look at any more of the books. It just hurt too much.

As she slid between the cold sheets of her queen-sized bed, she thought maybe she would give it one more try. Daniel said all she had to do was relax, open her mind, and leave the stress of the world behind. Quinn hoped this time it would work. She was beyond her breaking point and really needed to escape her current reality for a bit, even if for just a few hours.

Quinn settled back in the pillows piled high on her bed and closed her eyes. Pictures of her brother swirled through her mind. "You know, you're not making this very easy, little brother." She could almost hear his laughter softly tickle her ears. "I miss you so much, Danny. The colors of the world have all gone gray without you." Slowly she cleared her mind and concentrated on her breathing. As her body relaxed and her limbs melted into the mattress, she finally was able to do as Daniel told her to do. She let herself, all the sadness and pain, go. At last, the pain and melancholy that consumed her drifted away, and all that was left was blissful peace.

* * * *

The sun peeked through the filmy curtain covering the large glass doors on the ocean side of the bungalow. The salty ocean air tickled her nostrils and eased her awake. Quinn smiled to herself as she remembered how she got there. "Danny was right. If I put my mind to it, I *can* dream walk. I've no idea what island this is or where, but I love it!"

She moved over to the dressing table and slipped on a slinky purple sundress she found draped over the chair. Whoa! "Where did this come from, and how does it fit me?" She gazed at her svelte, tanned reflection and definitely loved what she saw. *If only I had this rocking bod back in the real world!*

Quinn moved out onto her deck to find coffee brewing along with a plate of fruit and a few pastries. She poured herself a large mug of the steaming joe, grabbed a cheese Danish, and headed for the beach. Walking barefoot in the sands along Lake Michigan as the water lapped against her calves had always relaxed her mind. She hoped the ocean would give her the same comfort. That's why she was there, after all, to relax and forget about everything for a bit.

"Quinn, hold up!"

She froze in her tracks.

No. It can't be.

Quinn slowly turned around, keeping her eyes closed. "Please don't let this be a cruel joke."

"It's not. Open your eyes, you goof. I'm really here."

"Danny!" She dropped her breakfast, flew into his arms, and held him tight as he spun her around. "I don't understand. How?"

"You should know better than to ask questions about that, darlin'. Nothing is impossible for the Big Man Upstairs, you know."

Quinn's smile faded a little bit. "What happened? Did I—"

"No! You're not dead. You finally cleared that busy brain of yours enough to relax and let yourself go in your dream world."

Her brother reached up and brushed some of her hair back behind her ear. She missed that. Her heart thudded. "What's wrong, Danny?" He always messed with her hair when he was trying to find a way to tell her something.

"Your visit here now is not just by chance. My partner, Michael, needs your help. His son's here and, well, we need you to convince him that life is worth living and to not stay on the Island."

"Why would I do that?" Quinn put her arms out and spun around in the sand. "This place is great. I just may stay here myself. Not like there's anything back there for me. I don't find the same joy in my work anymore. I can't listen to music without thinking about you and how you won't be around to have children of your own or to tour with your band. They had to choose another drummer, but they just don't sound the same without you. *I'm* not the same without you. Why not just stay here in this beautiful place and forget all the rest?"

Daniel's eyes flashed with anger, and Quinn took a small step back. "Don't you dare say that shit! You promised you would live for me, Quinn. There are people you haven't even met yet whose lives you'll change forever. Trust me."

"I don't know if I can believe that anymore. How can I help anyone when I don't even know who I am? When that drunk driver took you away from me, from our whole family, I stopped believing in miracles."

He wrapped his arms around her tight. "I'm here. Isn't that miracle enough for you? You brought yourself here, and that's a miracle, too. Do you understand how amazing that is in itself? You can come and go from this place at will as long as you don't abuse that gift. It's yours forever, and you can help so many people with it." He lifted her chin so she had to look into his eyes. "You're going to be given a rare chance here in this paradise. This will be the place where you meet your always and forever. Here you'll bind yourselves to each other, heart and soul. I promise this to you. Nothing and no one will keep you apart."

Quinn smiled through her tears and embraced her brother tight. "I see you're still the hopeless romantic."

He rested his chin on top of her head. "I'll let you in on another secret. I'm an even bigger romantic now if you can believe it. You aren't the only couple we have to watch over, you know."

"Are you saying we're just going to be able to leave this place together and walk off into the sunset for our happily ever after?"

Daniel shook his head. "It's not that cut and dry. You have to find each other again after you go back. When the time's right, you both will know."

"Figures. Things never can be straightforward, can they? There's always one more challenge to get through." Quinn sagged against Daniel's chest and sighed.

"Oh, come on! Where's your spirit of adventure? Aren't you the least little bit curious to find out who's your destiny?"

"Okay, okay. I guess I can meet this guy and see how it goes. What's his name?"

"Jacob. Jacob Michael Hartley."

* * * *

Lady Fate stood next to Michael, closely observing how Quinn reacted to her brother. "Our Daniel is very convincing, no?"

Michael turned to face the Goddess and smiled. Her emerald-green eyes sparkled and danced as her own smile lit up her already-glowing features. Her waist-length, curly red hair billowed in the tropical breezes of the Island, nearly taking his breath away with her beauty. "That he is. Without him, I don't think I'll be able to convince my son to go back."

Fate tilted her head slightly. "Both of them are going to give us some grief in that department, but this is the only way. They must seal their bond now so they can find each other soon thereafter. It's been a long and hard road for this couple, and I've been unable to intervene as much as I've wanted."

Michael lifted his eyebrows in surprise. "I don't understand. Couldn't you have made things easier for them before now?"

"No. Too many lives are woven together with those two. Certain paths must be chosen in order to get the results we want. These choices are not without consequences for someone. It takes time, sometimes several lifetimes, to get to the destiny foretold for them."

Michael still had trouble comprehending the intricacies of the goddess's powers. "But you're Fate. Don't you control Destiny?"

Her laugh jingled in his ears. "Well, I can only do so much. Yeshua has instilled free will into Our creations. He did that to prove to Lucius humans have the ability to be greater than all the others, including the original angels."

"Lucius has never liked humans much, has he?"

"That would be, as you say, an understatement. It's really not that he doesn't like them as much as he feels they're inferior and not deserving of the many blessings Yeshua wishes to bestow upon them. Lucius has had his own challenges to deal with lately. It's really quite amusing to see him want to pull his own hair out."

Michael chuckled. "Well, Daniel and I will keep working on these two and with the others of course."

The Goddess nodded. "As I know you will...along with that nudge here and there you're so good at." She winked and smiled once more.

Michael blushed. "Well, you didn't say we *couldn't* do that."

Lady Fate reached out and took his hand, squeezing it tight. "No, we did not. I've been known to nudge a bit myself from time to time, and so has Yeshua when he's felt it necessary to do so. Rest assured. Your charges will all end up with their true soul mates. The journey they must travel is filled with many obstacles and detours, but *all* of them will be stronger. Their love for one another will know no bounds, especially the love between Jacob and Quinn. Now is their time, and it's up to us to convince them they deserve it *and* one another."

CHAPTER 12

February 12, Las Vegas, Present Day

Quinn was shocked. She didn't really know what she expected to hear from Julia, but what she just said never crossed her mind. "Did you say because you could? What the hell does that mean?"

Julia's eyes locked with Quinn's. "I did everything back then because I could do it. No one told me no or denied me anything. I went from being a possession and sexual plaything for my parents to the one who had all the control. Unfortunately, I wasted too many years thinking that way of life made me happy. In truth, it did just the opposite." Julia bolted the rest of her wine down and continued. "If I didn't drive Jake away when I did, I would've taken him down that dark path with me. I had to force him to give up on me once and for all. That was the only way."

He stared at his ex and shook his head. "What do you mean the only way? I could've done without seeing you in bed with another man."

Julia closed her eyes and took a deep breath. Her body visibly shook. Quinn's heart went out to her. There was no way she was putting on an act. She needed to tell them the whole story and make them understand.

"I'm truly sorry you saw that. I was drunk and he drove me home. I never intended for that to happen in our home. It did, and I can't change that. My intention that night was to find some way to avoid meeting your mother. I knew she would see right through me and know I wasn't the one you needed in your life."

"If you felt that way, why didn't you tell me? It would've hurt like hell, but I could've handled that a hell of a lot better than what ended up happening. I wasn't the only one who got hurt. Kathy

Baker told me about the two of you that night. She was devastated finding out the man she loved was planning on marrying someone else."

Julia snorted. "I would never have agreed to marry that idiot. Believe me; he asked often. Mario Carlos had all sorts of grand plans. It had always been about image with him. He ended up treating me as his possession, and there was no way in hell I was going to live through that again. Kathy was so much better off without him, too. He screwed anything and everything that walked into the ER."

Quinn curiosity piqued. "If you didn't want any more to do with Mario, how did he end up driving you home?"

"I followed Jake to the bar."

"You did what?" Jacob ran his hands through his hair. "I didn't see you there."

"You were deep in conversation with Kathy. By her facial expressions, I knew she was telling you about seeing Mario and me in the supply closet. I panicked. I didn't want you to find out about any of that. I knew I had to break things off with you, but I wasn't ready. Instead of just going over there and talking to both of you, I ordered a drink. Then another and another. Next thing I knew, Mario was sitting next to me at the bar ordering me another round. You and Kathy were still talking to each other."

"So, Mario offered to drive you home and fuck you in our bed?"

"Jake!" Quinn squeezed his upper arm slightly. "Let her finish."

"He wanted to be sure I got home safe and sound, or so he said. He knew if he gave me enough booze, my no would turn into a yes. I was thinking if I drank enough, I would have the courage to let you go."

"Did you ever love me, Julia, or was it all just a game?" His voice was barely a whisper. This was the heart of it all. Quinn remembered how much they went through to be together. He had such a difficult time accepting she loved him unconditionally. His past with Julia was the key to all of it.

"I did care for you, deeply. Was it love? Yes, but was I in love with you? No. I tried to mold you into someone you weren't. You don't do that to the one who has your heart. It was and has always been Carmen. It took your accident to make me see that. If we stayed together, I would've made you miserable. The fact remains if I didn't cut you out of my life, you wouldn't have found Quinn. I was never the one for you, Jake. I knew that then and now. Seeing the two of you together tonight proves my point."

"We're right back to my original question. Why did we have to rehash this again? I nearly died in that accident. I spent years in rehab healing physically and mentally. I almost lost my chance to be with Quinn because of everything I went through with you. I managed to get through all of it because of her. I don't want to relive any of the misery."

The waiter arrived with their dinners before Julia could answer. Quinn held her tongue. She could feel the anxiety roll off of her husband in waves, but the only person who had the answers he needed was sitting across from them looking just as lost and alone as she had felt a few years ago. Quinn wished she had suggested they wait until Carmen was there to help support Julia. It had to be so hard for her to admit how horribly she had treated Jacob.

"In order for me to move forward in my life, it was important for me to tell you face to face what happened and why. I had to tell you I'm sorry for hurting you. Because you loved me the way you did, I was able to realize I didn't have to run away from my past any longer. I didn't need to hide behind a made-up persona. I could just be myself and not be the center of attention all the time. Because of your accident, I figured out what and who was really important to me. It was time I stopped running from the horrors of my childhood and finally put them to rest. It's taken all these years and one hell of a patient therapist to get me to this point today. I couldn't give my whole heart to anyone else, especially Carmen until I saw you again and asked if you could ever forgive me."

Jacob visibly relaxed and closed his eyes. "I forgave you long ago. Maybe it's time you finally forgive yourself and be happy with Carmen."

Quinn couldn't be prouder of Jacob at that moment even if she tried. Letting go of the past wasn't an easy thing to do, especially one full of so much pain. He finally recognized how important it was for Julia to have his blessing to be with the person she'd loved all of these years. "We could tell from her letter. Carmen has loved you for a very long time."

Julia smiled brightly. "It's over twenty-five years now she's been by my side, allowing me to work through everything and find myself. She's the one who has always had my heart. I didn't know it then, but

I do now. I had never been one of those people who believed in soul mates or love at first sight. I thought that was just something you found in romance novels. Seeing the two of you together tonight has given me a renewed hope for the future. How did the two of you meet, by the way?"

Jacob smiled for the first time that evening. "I'm not sure you'd believe our story if we told you."

"Oh, I don't know, Jake. Try me. You might be surprised by what I believe in nowadays."

CHAPTER 13

Thirteen Years Ago

"Hello? Is anyone home?" Jacob walked up the steps and onto the top deck of the bungalow just down the beach from his. An instrumental version of one of his favorite songs, the Righteous Brothers' "Unchained Melody," was playing inside. Whether or not this was the right place, he liked the occupant's taste in music.

As he reached out to knock on the half-opened glass door, she appeared. "You must be Jacob. My brother told me to keep an eye out for you tonight. I was hoping your dad would make an appearance, too. Danny's told me a lot about both of you."

He took her hand to shake it and was nearly knocked off his feet. The jolt that zipped through his body as soon as they touched surprised the shit out of him. He swallowed hard a few times in an attempt to hide his shock. Her eyes widened. *Did she fell it, too?*

"You must be Quinn. Please. Call me Jake." Jacob was once again rooted to the spot by mesmerizing eyes. He concluded they had to be a family trait, but hers elicited a whole different reaction in him, deep down in his soul. Something else drew him to her. He didn't understand why but was suddenly filled with an overwhelming surety he'd known her in another life or two.

Quinn smiled and guided him toward the table, still holding his hand. "I hope you're hungry. They've got the best fruit here, so I chose an assortment for a salad. I waited to put the steaks on, though. We wouldn't want to overcook those."

"No, we wouldn't want to do that." He could look into her eyes for hours, those come-fuck-me eyes people read about in *Playboy*. Here he was looking right into two of them now, and his mind wandered to that what-if zone. *Get a grip, Hartley!*

She smiled once again, and her entire face glowed. Jacob's heart skipped a couple of beats.

What the fuck is happening to me?

The sound of her voice brought him back from his fantasy. "I'm sorry. I can't stop staring into your eyes. I've never seen any so blue."

It was Jacob's turn to smile and blush. "I was going to mention something about yours, blue green like the ocean. I can't say I haven't seen those before. Your brother—"

"Danny and I share the same color. Our sister Miranda's are a little more on the blue side like our mother. I'll just go ahead and take a wild guess you have your father's eyes."

Jacob sat down with Quinn at the table and nodded. "I'm surprised you haven't met him yet. He isn't usually the one to shy away from meeting a beautiful woman."

She blushed deeply and rolled her eyes at him over her water glass. "Is that so?" She cleared her throat, moved forward in her chair, and rested her elbows on the table. "I thought I was the only one here until I saw my brother this morning on the beach. He told me we needed to meet tonight."

"My father said the same to me. Apparently, our dinner date is supposed to bring me one step closer to figuring out what I want to do with my life."

"Danny said they needed help to convince you to go back."

"Now why would I want to do that? I got great food, great company, and all on a beautiful tropical island."

"I couldn't agree with you more. Now that I'm finally here, I'm not so sure I want to go back either."

* * * *

"Hmm. Maybe it wasn't such a good idea to bring them together here or tell them they're destined to be together." Daniel's eyes widened and took the whole scene. "Fate said this time together for them would seal their bond, but all I see is them falling for each other now and forgetting they have to go back. If Jake and Quinn choose to be together here only, they'll forfeit their one chance to be together forever. They can't give up on life. Not now. Not ever."

Michael put his hand on Daniel's shoulder. "Be patient, my friend. Lady Fate also said these two have loved each other through many lifetimes and have been torn apart repeatedly. Now *is* their time. We just have to keep watch and give a nudge now and then. You know that pesky free will gets in the way every time!"

Both laughed loudly, not concerned they could be heard by Jacob or Quinn. The angels only revealed themselves when it was absolutely necessary.

In the case of Quinn and Jacob, there was no way they would be able to get the two of them on the right paths without materializing. For the others under their care, they were able to use other humans to help move things along. Daniel realized they were going to need to call in a few more humans to help with these two. Kathy was the perfect choice to stay with Jacob and his family in the hospital, but now the Guardians needed someone they could trust to watch over Quinn while she was out of her body, too.

"What ya thinking about, Danny?"

"Kathy's in place watching over your son. We need someone similar for my sister."

"Agreed. Anyone come to mind?"

Daniel nodded. "I've got the perfect human guardian to watch over Quinn. My cousin Brigid. She's a Wiccan priestess and would be the best candidate for the job. We can trust her completely. Care to meet her?"

"I can't wait. If she's anything like you and your sister, I'm going to enjoy myself immensely."

"You don't know the half of it. The last time I checked, she had short purple hair and had graduated first in her class from culinary school. If she wasn't already busy enough, she's singing with a heavy metal band, too."

Michael chuckled. "She sounds like a firecracker to me! Does she have any tattoos?"

Daniel laughed. "Several. Brig was one of the first people who sat in the chair at my station in my buddy's tattoo parlor. It wasn't too long before I covered her back with ink."

Michael smiled. "Let me guess, dragons?"

Daniel winked at his partner. "How about I let Brigid show them to you and you can see for yourself. She'd be more than a bit miffed if I stole her thunder."

* * * *

"You're right. The fruit here is wonderful, or maybe it's the company that gives it that extra-special pop?" He winked, and her face flushed.

"What did I say?"

"Oh, I was just thinking of something my sister told me about eating certain kinds of fruits." She bit her lower lip and stared at her plate a few seconds, avoiding his eyes, but kept smiling.

Jacob's own smile grew. He had an idea what she was referring to, but he wanted to hear her say it. "How about I put the steaks on? You can tell me what your sister had to say and what we can do with the information." He got up and leaned over to brush stray hairs behind her ear with his fingertips. "Your blush brings out the color in your eyes even more."

"Oh, now stop it! You're just teasing me." She stood up to help with the steaks but instead ended up standing just inches from him. Her voice dropped a few octaves as she chided him further. "Didn't your mother ever tell you it's not nice to tease a girl like that?"

He grazed his fingertips over her tanned cheek, finding it warm and still flushed. "Is that what we're doing here? You're the one bringing up the fruit all the time and not giving me a hint about what your sister told you about it." He, too, lowered his voice to just about a whisper. "Teasing? I prefer the terms flirting or enticing." He caressed her lips softly with his own. "Or even…seducing."

He leaned in to deepen the kiss. Her hands trailed up his arms, his neck, and then entwined in his hair. He pulled her close, molding her body to his. The feel of her in his arms brought everything full circle—as if he had always held and kissed her this way. Jacob didn't understand why he was with her, but he just knew he was simply supposed to be.

She broke the kiss and appeared to him to be just as surprised and at ease with him as he with her. "What about the steaks? We'll need to take them out to get to room temperature before we put them on the grill."

"They'll keep. I've got a pretty powerful craving for more of your fruit."

* * * *

"Well, I think that's our cue to disappear." Michael smiled broadly at his young partner. "You really don't want to watch what's going to happen next, do you?"

Daniel rolled his eyes. "I think I can do without the mental picture of my sister and your son in bed together, thank you very much. Besides, we need to check in on the others."

"It's time we see how the boys are doing convincing Stephen Eischer to undergo another round of chemotherapy."

"He's another stubborn mule. Lady Fate said the Big Guy has plans for him, so not going through with the chemo really isn't an option. It's going to be one hell of a show watching this all play out. I'm not so sure I'm going to be able to stand back and not give a few extra nudges along the way to all of them."

Michael smiled. "We won't be alone in this, you know. Our families will be there to help Jake and Quinn find their way to each other in the real world. I, for one, can't wait to see the love sparks fly between all of the couples we're watching over. At first glance, some of the pairings have surprised me and may require a bit of work to be sure all goes as planned."

Daniel tilted his head and rolled his eyes, making Michael chuckle once again.

"Okay, okay. I'll help with the extra nudging to be sure everyone follows their hearts. Let's stop in to see your cousin first. I've never seen anyone with purple hair before, and you've got me very intrigued about the ink you put on her back!"

The angels' forms slowly faded away into the ocean mist, leaving Jacob and Quinn completely alone together for the very first time.

CHAPTER 14

February 12, Present Day

Jacob searched Julia's face in an attempt to figure out what she thought of their story so far. "I told you it's a wild story, but every bit of it's true."

She leaned forward, put her elbows on the table, and rested her chin on her folded hands and smiled. "Your Guardian Angels helped you find each other on the Island ten years before you actually met here in Vegas? On the dance floor of Saints and Sinners?"

Quinn laughed. "Hard to believe it was only three years ago we found each other again. After my brother Danny died, I kept coming here year after year for the veterinary conference and searching for who knows what. I finally had the career going the way I wanted, but my heart still yearned for my dream lover."

"It must have been amazing to find each other like that and be able to start your life together knowing you were meant to be." Julia sighed and winked. "What an amazing gift from Fate."

Jacob smiled broadly. "Oh, we weren't able to be together right from that first moment. Both of us were going in other directions, and as I recall, Quinn's brother Derek threatened to beat the living shit out of me if I went near her during that visit."

"I almost forgot about that. He was a bit protective of me then and thought I'd be better off with someone more stable."

"Little did he know then *that* particular someone would play the key role in getting us down the aisle."

Julia's eyes widened. "Who did he want you to be with instead of your one and only?" She looked between the two of them, waiting for an answer. "Wait a minute. All the artwork at the club features you. I just played it off thinking you did Derek a favor by posing, but no."

Quinn shook her head. "I didn't pose for that painting at all. Derek originally did the portrait as a tattoo."

"Stephen Eischer? He's the one you're referring to, the one who helped the two of you get together?"

"That he did. He realized right away we were soul mates. At one point he told me if I didn't wake up and claim what was already mine, he was going to do everything in his power to win her for himself." Jacob leaned over and kissed Quinn softly. "I'm so happy I finally came to my senses and stopped feeling I wasn't worthy of loving you."

"Me, too, honey." Quinn smiled. "More and more of our time on the Island has been coming back to both of us now."

"Oh, please tell me more. I'm fascinated by your story. Not only did you meet and fall in love with Jake here in Vegas, but you managed to get one of the richest men in the world to fall for you, too. I have to say, I can completely understand how that happened. You're very beautiful. I would've chased after you myself back then."

Quinn blushed from the top of her head to her toes as Jacob laughed again. "Now there's a bit of the old Julia, flirting with my wife. You're shameless as ever." Their laughter rang through the restaurant as he signaled to the waiter to bring them another round of drinks. "There's still more to our story on the Island if you care to hear it."

She nodded and wiped a stray tear from her eye. "I would be honored to hear the rest of it."

Jacob reached across the table and covered Julia's hand with his. "I don't think I've ever heard you laugh that hard. I'm honored to finally meet the real you."

"It feels great to be able to be me around anyone, especially you and now your beautiful wife. I wish Carmen could be here for this. She won't believe half of this story when I tell her. The parts about the Guardian Angels will make her smile though."

"Why is that? Doesn't she share your belief in them?" Quinn leaned a little closer to Jacob.

His heartbeat quickened as the scent of her perfume filled his nose and another part of his anatomy stirred. She squeezed his thigh, letting him know she was more than aware of what she was doing to him. He was going to have so much fun getting even with her later in the suite after the twins were put down for the night.

"Actually, she was the believer right from the beginning. It took me a little more time to see the light, so to speak." She sat up quickly in her chair and crossed her arms on the table. "You just never mind about me and my beliefs in the angelic realm. I want to hear more about your Guardians and how they got you off the Island and into each other's arms."

CHAPTER 15

Thirteen Years Ago

"I was hoping you'd say that about the fruit I mean."

Jacob smiled. "Are you ever going to tell me what your sister had to say about the fruit?" He held her gaze as they stood just inches apart on the deck, the balmy ocean breeze gently tossing her hair off her bare shoulders. Jacob longed to reach out and sweep the rest of her hair from her neck while his lips found their way to her skin.

Quinn took his hands in hers and led him toward the open door of her bungalow. She licked her lips as her cheeks turned a deeper shade of rosy red. "Randi said certain foods can make a person's cum taste differently. I've never tried it before myself—"

"There's always a first time." Jacob's voice nearly gave out on him as he realized they were now standing in her bedroom. Much like with his accommodations, her master suite had the only access to the patio and the beach. His body trembled as the subtle fragrance of her perfume tickled his nose. Being so close to her and not holding her in his arms was damn near killing him. The music on the stereo in another part of the bungalow changed and Tim McGraw and Faith Hill sang their ballad "I Need You." Now was his chance.

Jacob pulled her arms up to wrap around his neck as they danced to the haunting tune. The soulful longing and love both singers had for each other poured out with each verse and tugged at his heart. He had never felt this way before, and yet it felt so right, as if it was always like this with her, his woman, his mate. His lips found hers once again, warm and welcoming. Quinn's tongue slipped and slid over his, drawing him in deeper and testing his control to the limit. Jacob desired her with every fiber of his being. He was torn between the need to take her right then and there and the desire to slow down and enjoy every moment they had together.

He picked her up and carried her to the California King in the center of the room. Laying her on the pillows at the top of the bed, he broke their kiss long enough to flip off his sandals and stretch out next to her. Quinn wrapped her arms around him as his body covered hers. Her fingers traced the muscles of his back as his lips trailed down her neck, nibbling, kissing, and tasting along the way.

Her breasts appeared to be straining against the bodice of her sundress. Jacob flicked his tongue into the deep cleft between them, eliciting a moan from Quinn. He held her gaze as he pushed the thin straps of the dress off of her shoulders. He used his teeth to tug at the strings keeping her shuddering tits in place. She giggled as her dress slowly opened up to him. The sound tickled his stomach. Jacob craved that sound and promised to do everything in his power to hear her giggle, laugh, and cry out for him over and over again.

* * * *

Oh my God, this man is hot! Quinn's body burned with desire. Just the scent of him made her body react immediately. From the moment she heard his voice, her lacy panties were wet. Trying to take in everything about him all at once sent every one of her senses into overdrive. His eyes, his skin, his scent, every little thing caused her body to shiver with wanton need. When he touched her, it was as if she was zapped with electricity and her mind went to mush. All she kept thinking about was leading up to this moment there with him in her bed.

His eyes found hers and she lost the last of her restraint. She let go and fell into him. She didn't care. Thoughts of going back or staying there on the Island disappeared. All she wanted to think about, to feel, and to taste was him. She pulled his mouth back to hers. The sweet taste of the berries, mango, and papaya dazzled her taste buds as their tongues teased and danced with each other, fighting for control one moment and surrendering to each other the next.

Jacob finally freed her tits from the laces of her bodice. Watching him tug at the strings with his teeth made her heart beat faster, and she giggled before she could stop. He winked and kept up the slow pace. Quinn giggled even more. "I stand by my first assessment. You're a tease, Jake."

"Baby doll, you haven't seen anything yet." He pushed her dress down to her waist and simply stared. "I'm not the only tease here."

"What are you talking about?" Quinn slid her fingertips up and down his arms. His muscles twitched and pulsed at her touch. She wanted those arms wrapped around her and to never let go.

"You are the most beautiful woman I've ever met. You don't flaunt it, but every move and noise you make turns me on. I wanted to take this slow, but I can't."

"Stop thinking so much and kiss me." She pushed herself up to meet his mouth as they moved on the bed so she was now on top of him. Jacob's hands slid up her thighs, leaving hot trails with his fingertips. Her body quaked and her pussy clenched as a rush of fluid soaked her panties completely.

Jacob hooked his thumbs in the band of her underwear, snapped them off, and tossed them onto the floor. His hands slid up her body, pulling the dress up and over her head in a flash. He sat up, holding her in his lap, nuzzling first one breast and then the other with his stubbly chin and cheeks. The roughness of his skin against her rock-hard nipples sent her rolling toward an orgasm. She clung to him as he suckled harder on her right nipple while kneading her left breast with his hand. Quinn arched her back and bit her lip before crying out. "Jake, please don't—"

He pulled back quickly, moving his hands to cradle her face. Concern filled his eyes. "Did I hurt you?"

Her eyes glistened with tears. "No. Please don't stop."

* * * *

The catch in her voice nearly broke his heart. The raw passion was there. She gave her body freely to him, and yet she still questioned his desire for her. He knew that pain all too well. Here with Quinn though, it all faded away. She did that for him, and he wanted so badly to do the same for her. He wiped away the tears that spilled onto her flushed face. He kissed her softly and held her close. "I want you, now and for however long we can be together. I need to be with you. I won't stop as long as you want the same."

Quinn slid off his lap and knelt up on the bed, pulling him up with her. She held his gaze as her fingers unfastened his shorts and then slid them down over his hips. Jacob quickly took off his tank top before crushing Quinn's chest against his. She smiled, and his heartbeat quickened. "I need you, too. Make love with me, Jake."

He stepped out of his shorts as Quinn eased back onto the pillows. Jacob took in her entire sun-kissed body, naked before him. *God, she's so beautiful.* Quinn welcomed him into her arms as he joined her on the pillows, his mouth finding her left nipple this time as his right hand trailed down her stomach.

She arched her back and moaned as soon as his fingers found her throbbing clit. Another wave of fluid gushed out of her and over his fingers. Jacob brought them up to his mouth to taste her. "Mmmm. You taste fucking fantastic. Your sister was right. Wanna try?"

Quinn giggled and licked his fingers clean. That move sent his body over the edge. His cock bounced with his need for her, a fact that didn't go unnoticed by his lover. She reached inside the nightstand for the box of condoms, spilling several over the bed. Jacob smiled as he placed one in her open palm. Quinn slid her hands down his abs to his pulsing member. She wrapped her fingers around his shaft and squeezed a little, eliciting a gasp from him. Carefully she tore open the wrapper with her teeth and covered his cock with the ribbed latex sheath.

He thrust his hips forward, causing her hand to slide up and down his shaft. "Oh, now who's teasing?" Jacob moaned.

He eased Quinn all the way back onto the pillows and slid down her body toward his prize. He wanted more than just a taste. He wanted to feast on her cunt until she begged for him to take her. He positioned himself between her thighs and looked up to see her watching him, her chest rising and falling rapidly. He popped her clit into his mouth and sucking hard. Quinn nearly bucked him off, but he held her hips in place, enjoying her squirming and sighs. It wasn't long at all before he was rewarded once again with her sweet nectar.

He teased her with his tongue and slipped one, two, and then three fingers inside of her hot folds. Her pussy clenched repeatedly over his fingers and her body convulsed over and over again. Quinn's skin flushed from her tits to her toes, because of him, because of what he was doing to her. He wanted more, so much more. He couldn't wait any longer. He wanted to bury his cock deep inside her, go over the edge, and never come back.

* * * *

He slid up her body and guided her legs up to wrap around his waist as he teased her clit with the head of his cock. "Jake, Jake, now, baby. Take me now." He slid into her slowly, her body adjusting to his size easily, contracting and pulling him in deeper until he completely impaled her.

Quinn's mind raced to catch up to her body. No one had ever elicited this kind of response from her. Every touch, every kiss left her body begging for more.

Her thighs tightened around him as he stroked her pussy, slow and steady at first, gradually picking up his pace and taking Quinn through one orgasm after another. Just as one zipped through her, another hit hot on its heels. She couldn't think. She couldn't speak. She could barely breathe but still begged for more of him.

He slid his hands up her arms, pinning them above her head. She braced her feet on the bed as Jacob continued to pound her now, her double-D-cup breasts bouncing wildly with each thrust. "Take me with you, baby."

Jacob's whispered plea triggered another violent eruption. His cock exploded within her as they came together one last time. He collapsed on top of her, releasing his hold on her hands over her head. She wrapped her arms around his body as he rolled them over onto their sides.

He rested his forehead against hers as their breathing slowed and became a bit more regular. She smoothed some of his long brown hair back off of his forehead and rested her palm against his cheek. "What the hell just happened?" She searched his eyes for any answers and found the same confusion she was feeling, along with something more. In his deep-blue eyes, she found peace and recognition. This was the man who would forever hold her heart.

"I don't understand it any more than you do. There was an immediate connection between us as soon as I looked into your eyes and again when we touched for the first time. I've never believed something like this could really happen. God help me, I think I've fallen in love with you."

"Oh, Jake, I love you, too. What are we going to do?" She should be overjoyed but was instead surprised by the angry feelings flooding through her now. How could Fate be so cruel as to give her this love when he was near death in the real world? Was this supposed to happen this way, or were they just to keep each other company until they both were ready to go back?

"Well, if we can't be together after we go back, then I'm not going. It's simple as that. I finally found the one person that makes me feel—"

"Whole." Quinn placed her hand over Jacob's heart. "In your heart, you feel whole as if you finally found a part of you that was missing."

Jacob covered her hand with his. "Exactly. Unless your brother and my pop can convince me that we'll find each other again if I go back, I choose to stay here with you for as long as possible."

* * * *

Quinn eased herself down into the hot tub, closed her eyes, and sighed. "Now this is heaven!"

Jacob laughed. "Not sure how I should take that." He splashed her, eliciting another round of giggles.

She splashed back and settled against the spa pillow. "Oh, you know what I mean. You've given my whole body a workout, and I need to loosen up if we're going to keep this up." Jacob reached down, grabbed her feet, and placed them on his lap. He slowly massaged each toe before moving on to her instep. "Good Lord! You keep doing that and I'm going to completely melt in here."

"That's the idea, honey. Gotta keep you all relaxed and putty in my hands."

She opened one eye and peered at him. "And why is that?"

He smiled slowly, tilting his head to the side, never stopping the foot massage that now had Quinn fighting for control. She knew he was putting on the charm now, but she wasn't about to complain one bit. Any man who could rub her feet like that had her full attention. Well, at least until his hands started to roam. Then all bets would be off.

"I was hoping you'd tell me more about why you needed to be here. I mean, I was near death. What made you want to escape your life?"

Her stomach did a little flip. It definitely wasn't the gut wrenching she would normally experience when anyone asked how she was doing. She felt so at ease with Jacob. Maybe it was time she talked about it all. "Around 2:30 a.m. this last Thanksgiving, Danny was killed by a drunk driver."

"He told me you were having a rough time with his passing." Jacob's fingers moved up her calves, working out all of the kinks and busting through all of her walls at the same time. For the first time since Daniel died, she felt safe enough to open up and talk about her loss.

"Rough time? Yeah, I guess you could say that. For the first week, I was completely numb. I refused to believe he was gone. I mean, it had to be a huge mistake or a cruel joke. There was no way my baby brother was dead. They wouldn't let us see his body because he was too mangled. We had to have a closed casket, and somehow it all just seemed like a bad dream, a horrible nightmare I was going to wake up out of in the morning. Well, the nightmare never ended for me. I saw his face and heard his voice everywhere.

"He was riding his motorcycle in the freezing rain and snow that commonly falls this time of year in Michigan. I wasn't worried about him on that bike. He was always a very safe driver. It's the other yahoos on the road that scared me to death every time he got on the back of his Harley." She turned away a moment and wiped the tears from her cheeks before she could continue. "This man, with his family in the car mind you, crossed the center line going nearly 100 miles an hour. Not only did he put his own life in danger, he put the lives of his children on the line simply because he wouldn't hand the keys over to his wife. He hit Danny head-on and dragged him for nearly five miles before he stopped. Here's the real kicker. If it wasn't for a few other witnesses, he would've fled the scene. Three guys tackled him to the ground, all the while having to fight off his wacky wife. The police arrested both of them at the scene. Both of them claimed it was my brother's fault."

Jacob's hands froze. He looked to Quinn as if he'd seen a ghost. All the color had drained from his face. "I know it's gruesome, Jake. I'm sorry to be so matter-of-fact."

"It's not that. I really don't know how to say this other than to just put it out there. I was on my bike when I had my accident, too. It just doesn't seem right to me that I got this second chance and not your brother."

Quinn shook her head. "If you had said that to me a few weeks ago, I would've agreed with you, but not now. So many things in our lives are out of our control. Just because I wish to have my brother alive and well doesn't make it so. I have to learn to accept we all have our own destinies. Danny's seems to be as a Guardian Angel."

"Well, he got the two of us together now. I'd say he's off to a great start." Jacob slid across the tub and behind Quinn, wrapping his arms around her tightly. "The two of you must have been very close."

She leaned her head back against his chest. "Our whole family's close, but Danny and I were two peas in a pod. From the moment he could walk, he was my little shadow, and I loved it. Even as a little guy, he loved colors and music. He could play the guitar by the time he was five, but the drums? Now there was his passion! He was always practicing and eventually writing his own songs. The guys that were in the band before Danny died had all been together since they were in middle school. It broke my heart to watch them try to play on without him. They were hurting nearly as much as I was, but I just couldn't be around them. It hurt too much."

Jacob nodded against her cheek. "Losing my pop last year knocked me for a loop, too. He was the guiding force of our family. He always told me I would find my way some day. He never compared us to each other, but I felt inadequate next to Eric and Maredyth. They had clear ideas of what they wanted out of life. I didn't have a clue, still don't really."

"That's nothing to be ashamed of, Jake. When you find your passion, you'll know it."

He kissed her forehead and held her even tighter. "I'm beginning to believe that now."

Quinn laughed. "Nothing like a couple of angels to show you the way, is there?"

"Well, they are pretty convincing." Jacob nibbled on her earlobe before trailing kisses down her neck to her shoulder. "If we're destined to be together, why can't we find each other right away? Why do we have to be apart at all?"

Quinn slid her hands slowly over Jacob's arms. "I don't know. It doesn't seem fair, but then again how many people get to spend time with their soul mates long before they actually meet?"

"You got a point there, baby doll. Until we have to part, I intend to explore every inch of you over and over again."

She turned to face him, taking his face in her hands before kissing him deeply. "Let's go inside and get started on that now, shall we?"

CHAPTER 16

Daniel and Michael materialized to the left of the stage as the band finished their set. Cheers erupted as Brigid hit the last high note, holding it for well over ten seconds. Michael was impressed. The girl had some talented pipes, and just like the rest of Daniel's family, she was mighty fine on the eyes.

A smile flashed across her bloodred lips when she noticed the angels waiting for her. She took a few more bows with the band, thanking the crowd for coming out and sharing their last set. Apparently, tonight was Brigid's last hurrah with the musicians. Daniel had told him she was getting too busy graduating from culinary school and starting up a catering business with another family friend.

"Well, well, well. Who did you bring with you tonight, Danny?" Brigid's silver eyes sparkled from the lights still flashing on the stage. "I haven't seen you in a few days. I was beginning to wonder if the Goddess planned to keep you all for Herself!"

Daniel laughed. "She does keep both of us hopping." He hugged her tightly and began the introductions. "Brig, this is my partner, Michael Hartley. Sarge, this is my cousin, Brigid Moon."

Michael smiled and shook her hand. "Ms. Moon, you have an amazing voice. If you can cook half as well as you sing, well, let's just say I'd like to introduce you to my youngest son."

"If he's half as good looking as you, introduce away, Mr. Hartley. Introduce away!" Brigid's bawdy laughter brought smiles to people all around them. Michael included. He found himself completely smitten with the dark-purple-haired pixie.

"Please call me Brigid."

"As long as you call me Michael, you have a deal." They shook on it once again.

Daniel put his arm around his cousin as they made their way to the back of the club and the stairwell leading up to her apartment. "You know I love visiting with you, but we do have another reason for being here tonight."

"Let me guess. You want my help with Quinn and her quest for her soul mate?"

Michael's eyes widened. "You know about them?"

Brigid laughed again. "Being a Wiccan priestess has its perks. Besides getting visits from handsome angels, the Goddess blesses me from time to time as well. Oh, and then there's the occasional appearance from the dark and mysterious Lucius. He thinks he's being sly, but I know he's watching." She opened the door to her apartment and beckoned them inside. "Has Quinn mastered dream walking yet?"

"With a little help from me, she made it to the Island. She's there now trying to understand *why* she is there."

"And who's watching over her body while she's enjoying the sun and fun?" Brigid cracked open a bottle of water and gulped down half of it. "She can't be there much longer without assistance. Before long, her body will weaken and diminish in this world. If it fades too far, she'll be on that island forever."

Daniel nodded. "That's why we're here. There isn't anyone else we can trust to watch over her. Quinn needs the time to bond with Jacob before they leave the Island. We have to convince them they'll find each other again, so Christmas morning we're going to bring them back to their bodies."

Brigid nodded. "Okay. Count me in. Where's Jacob's body, if you don't mind me asking?"

Michael winced. "He's in a hospital in Los Angeles. He nearly died in an accident while riding his Harley."

Daniel locked eyes with his cousin. "I know what you're thinking, Brig. I miss you guys, too. I'm fulfilling my destiny now. Shouldn't Jake get the chance to do the same?"

She nodded and hugged him. Michael was touched by how much they cared for each other. He knew how hard it was for him to leave his own family, but Daniel had only been gone for a month. His family had to still be reeling from their loss.

"Just give me a few minutes to pack my bags and I'll head over to Quinn's place tonight. I still have the spare key she gave me when she went to that vet conference last year." She peeled off her leather jacket and stood in front of them in her miniskirt, fishnets, and leather corset. For the first time that night, Michael was able to see some of the tattoos covering her body.

"Danny? Did you do that entire piece on Brigid's back all by yourself?"

"He did all of them. I was his very first guinea pig." She winked. "Don't you just love the flight of the Fae?" She turned around so he could get a closer look at the various images.

"They're beautiful, and they look so real. I can almost see their wings move." There were a dozen fairies in flight covering her back. So many colors danced in front of his eyes. Michael had never seen tattoos look so alive before. "Daniel, my friend, your work's truly amazing."

Daniel laughed. "Thank you. If you appreciate mine, wait until you see more of Derek's work. The portraits alone will make you weep. Lady Fate asked me to watch over him while he was setting up his tattoo parlor in the MGM Grand. I would have loved to learn some of his techniques with shading. I was just starting to learn how to do portrait tats from one of my mentors before I died."

Michael touched his partner's shoulder. He knew how hard it was for him just after his own death. There were more than a few thoughts of what could have been. Maybe one day Daniel would be given a second chance at life as a human, but until then they had a job to do now. "I have to admit. I thought with your interest in dragons, Brigid would have at least part of her body adorned with one."

"Oh, I do." She lifted her skirt to expose her bare upper thigh and the deep-crimson dragon in flight. "Dragons and dragonflies are my spirit guides."

Michael whistled. "If these were some of your first tats, I can understand why you were in such demand. Amazing. Simply amazing."

Brigid kicked her heels off. "Okay, I think we've contributed to my cousin's big head enough for one night." The angels laughed with her. "Give me fifteen minutes and I'll be ready to head over to Quinn's condo." She stopped in her tracks and stared at Daniel. "What the hell am I supposed to tell your mother? She's going to ask a lot of questions, specifically why Quinn hasn't called. You know how she is. She won't stop until she gets the answer she wants."

Daniel shrugged. "I'm sure you'll think of something."

"Gee, thanks." She tossed one of the couch pillows at him. "I'll have to pull the Wiccan card."

Michael was confused. "I don't understand. What's the Wiccan card?"

"Christmas isn't the only holiday this season. For me and my fellow pagans, it's the Winter Solstice. As a priestess, I have rituals to perform. Fortunately, or unfortunately for us, my aunt Helen is very open minded and has no issue with my religion. She just wants me there for dinner!"

"How about promising her both you and Quinn will visit after your rituals? That should give us enough time to get everything done on the Island, don't you think?" Michael's mind raced. "Time moves faster there than it does here. They can only stay there a couple weeks, so both of them will be back by New Year's Day. That's the deadline given to us by The Three."

Both Brigid and Daniel stared at him in silence. Michael almost second-guessed his suggestion until Daniel nodded and smiled broadly.

"That's perfect. I know my ma just wants the family to all be together as much as possible this month. She's so worried about Quinn, and she'll actually be relieved to hear she's participating in the Solstice rituals."

"Don't you worry about a thing, Danny. I'll come up with something to stall your mother. You two make sure that Quinn and Jake get back to their bodies on Christmas."

* * * *

Kathy sat back and let the patients tell Eric their stories. A few times, she caught him wipe a tear from his eye and laugh out loud at some of their tales. "Eric, did James tell you how long he was in his coma before he woke up?"

James didn't skip a beat. "I was out for almost six months. Just about everyone gave up on me, but not the team here. My tests kept showing I was in there, you know? I couldn't speak, but I could hear them talking. It was Kathy who was a godsend. She helped my wife understand what was happening to me. Because of her, my family held on and let me come back when I was ready."

Eric smiled. "Are you telling me my brother can hear us when we talk to him?"

All the patients in their circle nodded. James reached out and grasped his shoulder. "I'm telling you he can hear you and *understand* everything you say to him and around him. He just can't show you yet. Have faith in your brother if nothing else."

Kathy knew she made the right choice to bring Eric down to meet her former patients. She had sensed his faith was failing him and he needed a boost. Hopefully, it was enough to keep him from feeling he let his brother down by keeping him on the machines. "Each and every one here had family members who were in your shoes, Eric. They all got through it and are here today because they're fighters. Jake's one, too. Trust in that."

Eric stood up and shook hands with everyone. "Thank you for sharing your stories with me. Knowing he can hear us when we talk to him does make it easier to see him hooked up to all those machines."

James stood up and took him in a bear hug. "Trust in your heart. Miracles happen every day. All of us here got our miracles and our second chances. Who's to say your brother won't get one, too?"

Kathy looked beyond Eric and James to find Michael leaning against the wall, smiling. He gave her the thumbs-up sign and slowly fading out of sight. She heard his voice in her ear a moment later.

"Good idea to bring him here. Thank you, Kathy." She put her hand over her heart and nodded. Working with the angels still gave her a bit of a rush, but knowing they really existed somehow made her job a little easier.

Eric waved his hand in front of her face. "Kathy? Where did you go?"

She laughed. "Oh, I was just talking to your Guardian Angel. It seems you Hartley boys are always giving him grief!"

All of the patients joined in laughing. Eric laughed hardest of all. "I bet he's going to need a nice long vacation if Jake comes out of this."

Kathy stared at him and smiled again. Eric was trying to keep the faith, and that was a good sign. "*When* Jake comes out of this, I'm sure a couple of angels will need some time off. Come on. Let's get some food into you and back upstairs to help get your brother ready for surgery."

"You really think he's stable enough to go through another surgery so soon?" Eric pushed the elevator button for the first floor. "I thought it depended on his results."

"Didn't you listen to what James said about miracles?" Eric smiled and nodded. "Well, I've got a feeling, Jake's miracle is due to happen any time now."

CHAPTER 17

February 12, Las Vegas, Present Day

Quinn sat back and listened to her husband tell Julia about the first time he tried to change diapers by himself. She could still picture it now. Jacob frantically reaching for another diaper as little Daniel discovered he could pee straight up in the air and hit his daddy in the eye. Not to be outdone by her brother, Stephanie grabbed the bottle of powder and shook it like mad, covering everyone in a blizzard of fine cornstarch.

"There we were covered in powder and Daniel shot more pee in the air. Both of them looked at me, and I swore they were going to start bawling and wake up Quinn, but no. Not my children. They giggled and giggled. The more I shook the powder out of my hair, the harder they laughed. It wasn't my finest hour as a parent, but I have to tell you, it was the most memorable."

Julia could barely breathe through her laughter. She held her hand up as a sign to give her a moment, but that only spurred Jacob on. "Oh, you think that's bad? Let me tell you what happened when I tried to clean them up!"

Quinn looked around at the other patrons in the restaurant, hoping their conversation wasn't disturbing anyone when she noticed Steve at the bar watching them with a sly smile on his face. Her cousin Brigid must have arrived early and relieved him of babysitting duties. She smiled and waved him over to their table. This night had turned out much better than she had ever hoped.

"From the look of things, I'd say your dinner meeting is a success." Steve's emerald eyes appeared to dance in the candlelight of the table.

Julia could only manage to nod through her laughter and motioned for him to take the seat next to her. When she could finally catch her breath, she filled him in. "They've been telling me a bit of what it's like to raise twin toddlers. For the life of me, I don't know how they do it. I'm exhausted just hearing the stories. But this last one with the picture of Jake standing there covered in baby powder and getting shot in the eye with pee was just too much."

Steve smiled broadly and signaled to the bartender to send his drink over to the table. "That's one of my favorite stories, too. I wish you guys had the nanny cam set up then. The video of that night would be priceless! Stephie and Danny are a handful, I'll grant you that, but also a joy. From the moment I held them in my arms for the first time in the delivery room, I've been head over heels in love."

"Wait? You were there when they were born?"

Jacob nodded. "Just about the entire family was there. The twins didn't want to be left out of the party and demanded to come into the world on our wedding day."

"They were kicking up a storm all day, but at least they waited until the reception to decide they wanted out. I was dancing when my water broke. Unbeknownst to me, Jake and Steve had a plan in place if that were to happen. Before I knew it, we were at the hospital and I was swearing up a storm."

Steve laughed. "You scared Jake enough he came out for reinforcements!"

Julia shook her head in amazement. "Wow! You two really have had a crazy life together after the Island."

"Oh, is that what you've been talking about tonight?"

"It's an amazing story. Imagine being able to meet your soul mate ten years before you actually lay eyes on each other here in Vegas. Have you two been able to go back since then?"

"There is one more visit we didn't tell you about yet." Jacob's eyes clouded over, and he reached for Quinn's hand, clutching it for dear life. Quinn squeezed his hand in return, hoping to reassure him everything was all right now.

Julia looked between the three of them and waited for an answer. "What? You look like you've seen a ghost, Jake."

Steve spoke up first. "We nearly lost both of them on that island two years ago."

"I don't understand? I thought it was all settled. Didn't you help them get together finally?"

Steve smiled and shrugged.

"That he did," Quinn spoke softly, still overcome by emotion after all this time. "He stuck by me after I had a nervous breakdown—"

"Because of me." Jacob's voice cracked, and he looked to his friend to bail him out.

Steve sipped his scotch and continuing the story. "Julia, these two were separated by circumstances a little out of their control. I admit, back then I wanted to have Quinn all for myself, but I knew the only one who would truly make her happy was Jake. She was the only one who could do the same for him. So instead of waiting for them to figure it out, I took matters into my own hands."

"I'm still lost." Julia's eyes bored into Quinn's. "When did you have a nervous breakdown?"

"About two months after I found out Jake was going to marry someone else."

"What?" Julia sat back heavily against her chair, unable to disguise her shock.

Jake nodded. "Yep. It wasn't the smartest move on my part, but I thought she'd be better off with Steve. He would give her everything I couldn't."

"Except her heart belonged to you and always did." Steve smiled and turned back to Julia to continue the story. "I took care of her the best I could and then told Jake to straighten up or I'd fight tooth and nail to keep her for myself."

"Holy shit! I think I need another drink, maybe a double."

Quinn laughed. "I told you our story is full of twists."

"You weren't kidding. So how did you nearly lose both of them on the Island?" She turned in her seat to face Steve, her gray eyes wide with expectation.

"This part is still a bit of a mystery to all of us, but it seems both traveled back to the Island in their dreams, searching for each other. Once they were there—"

"I didn't want to go back. There was too much pain, and I didn't want to live without her. Once I had her in my arms there in that paradise, I never wanted to let her go. I begged her to stay there with me forever."

Julia shook her head slowly and visibly paled. "But you couldn't do that. People here needed you in their lives."

Jacob stared at her for a few beats. "Exactly. As much pain as we were in, we couldn't put that off on those we loved. Instead, we spent every moment they allowed us to have together before we had to come back and fight for what was ours. How did you know that?"

Her eyes filled with tears. "It seems we have a lot more in common than I first realized. I made it to the Island, too, and some beautiful young hunk covered in tattoos told me I couldn't stay. I had too much living yet to do, with Carmen."

Quinn reached for Julia's hand across the table. "You met Danny?"

Julia nodded. "That's a story for another night if you don't mind. I would like to tell you all about it when Carmen's here. I've not told her the whole story yet either."

"It's a date." Quinn squeezed Julia's hand. A lot had happened to all of them through the years. She smiled to herself and thanked her brother for watching over them. It made her heart glad to know he had indeed found his calling as a Guardian Angel.

Julia wiped the last of the tears from her eyes and smiled once more. "What happened when you left the paradise the first time thirteen years ago? Did you have any memory of it at all then?"

"The first time? I freaked out that we didn't get enough time together but couldn't speak when I first woke up. I was still in the hospital hooked up to a respirator. It was Christmas Day as I recall."

Quinn nodded. "I remembered it all and of course panicked to find myself back in my bedroom in Michigan."

CHAPTER 18

Thirteen Years Ago

Even before her eyes opened, Quinn sensed something wasn't quite right. Her mind immediately flew into panic mode. *No! Please not yet!*

She sat up quickly, her heart beating erratically. Seeing the familiar surroundings of her bedroom in Auburn Hills would've normally made her relax. Instead, she wanted to scream. "Could all of it have been a dream? One big, cruel joke?"

"For someone with a scientific mind, you sure like to jump to conclusions without all the facts." Daniel leaned against the frame of her bedroom door, scowling and shaking his head.

Quinn flopped back down onto the pile of pillows she loved to keep on her bed. "Why did I have to come back now? Did we do something wrong?"

He sat down next to her and took her hands. "It's not what you're thinking. Neither one of you did anything wrong. Jake had to go back for a little bit, too. You've been asleep here for nearly thirty-six hours. You had to come back here in order to keep your body going. Otherwise, you'd be stuck on the Island." Quinn raised her eyebrows and was about to give a smartass remark, but Daniel silenced her with a tilt of his head. "That's not part of the plan, and you know it."

"Can I go back at any time?"

He nodded. "You can, and you will. Do you know what today is?"

Quinn shook her head. Out of the corner of her eye, she noticed the stack of Christmas cards on her nightstand. "Christmas? Ma's going to be pissed I haven't checked in yet."

Daniel chuckled. "Don't worry about that. Randi has her occupied with the three munchkins and getting ready for the whole clan to get together over the next few days. Brigid has been covering for you, too. She told Ma you were on a Winter Solstice retreat and would call them as soon as you had phone service."

"Good move using the Wiccan card, little brother." She moved to give him a high-five but stopped short and then narrowed her eyes slightly. "Wait a minute. Brig can see you, too? When did that happen?"

"Right from the start. She's become quite a powerful witch over the years, and you'd know that if you hadn't had your nose buried in your medical books all the time." Daniel flicked the tip of Quinn's nose, making her smile. "She's been able to see angels and other spirit creatures since we were kids."

"I always thought those were wonderful stories. It's not that I didn't believe she could see spirits. I didn't realize she could actually help me talk to you again…and…well, why the hell didn't she say something to me?"

"Oh, for Pete's sake! You've buried yourself in your work and cut yourself off from everyone. Brigid tried. *Everyone* has tried to talk to you. This is why I finally had to step in and help you with your dream walking. We hoped you'd figure it out on your own, but you kept denying your ability."

Quinn sighed and hugged her brother. "Okay, okay. You're right. I shut myself off from everyone. It just hurt too much."

"And now?"

"It still does but being with Jake has helped a lot." Her eyes widened and her cheeks began to burn. "How much do you know? I mean, were you watching the whole time?"

"Enough to know you've fallen in love with each other."

"Then let me go back to him. I haven't been able to convince him he has to leave the Island yet. What if he wakes up and finds me gone? What if he gives up?"

"Like you did?" Daniel held her gaze for a moment before turning away.

"What are you talking about?" Quinn once again flopped back on the pillows and stared up at the ceiling, avoiding her brother's piercing eyes.

"Both of you have to understand that in order for you to be together, you have to leave the Island willingly. You have to *choose* that path. Otherwise—"

"We lose each other again?"

Daniel nodded and pulled her back up into a sitting position. "What's it gonna be? The path that leads you to Jake, or the one where you go on and never hold him in your arms again in this lifetime?"

"Yes, Quinn. What *is* your choice?"

Quinn nearly jumped out of her own skin. She thought they were alone but should've known better. She'd know the vision before her anywhere. She'd seen her in her dreams for years. The Goddess Fate materialized before them, smiling and gesturing for Quinn to go on.

"There's only one choice for me."

"On the contrary, my child. There are multiple paths before you. Each one leads to a different future. People you meet on one path may not meet you if you choose another route. Your choices help to fulfill not only your destiny but that of others in this lifetime and the next."

Quinn stood up from the bed and knelt on the floor in front of Lady Fate. "Goddess, I choose Jacob. I choose our destiny together, whoever we meet along the way, and wherever that may lead."

"Very well." Fate smiled and emitted a bright light as her body slowly faded from the room. "Your brother will help you prepare things here so you can spend more time on the Island. You need to complete the bond with Jacob before you return to your separate lives. Remember, you *will* find each other again in no time at all." Her voice continued even though Quinn could no longer see her or her light. "Look for the sign of Our promise to you both. You will know it when you see it."

* * * *

Daniel helped Quinn get up from the floor. Her face radiated pure joy. He knew the feeling. He felt the same when he first met the

Goddess and then again when he was chosen to be Guardian over his family and others.

"She's even more beautiful than I've ever imagined, Danny." She giggled and hugged him before letting him go. "Well, what're we waiting for? Let's get cracking! I have calls to make before I go back. What else do I need to do?"

Daniel reached for her and hugged her tight to his body. "Promise you'll live for me, Quinn. Enjoy everything life has to offer, and that includes love, laughter, music, and art. Most of all, promise me you'll follow your heart no matter what."

Quinn pulled back and placed her hands on either side of his face. "I promise."

"So, what're we promising?"

Quinn jumped in his arms, making Daniel chuckle again. He loved surprising her, and this time was no exception. Both of them turned to greet the very sleepy-eyed, purple-haired, voluptuous beauty that was their cousin Brigid Moon.

"Brig! Did you see her?"

"The Goddess? Many times." Brigid smiled brightly. "I'm so happy you finally opened your eyes. She's been visiting you a lot, you know."

The puzzled expression on Quinn's face nearly had Daniel laughing once again, but he wisely held his tongue. "Why?"

Their cousin rolled her eyes. "Will you shut off the analytical part of your brain for just a little while and enjoy the moment?" Brigid hugged Quinn tightly before holding her at arm's length and twirling her around the room. "Why? Why not? Fate has plans for everyone. For her to directly intervene this way proves you hold the key to not only your own destiny but that of a few others as well."

Daniel agreed. "That's what we've been trying to get through to her all this time. Now that you're here, maybe she'll listen."

"Well, forgive me for finding all of this overwhelming." Quinn let go of her cousin's hands and stood with her arms crossed over her chest and her hip out to the side.

Daniel glanced quickly at the grinning Brigid. Both of them knew they were in for it now once Quinn took that particular stance. They had been privy to it numerous times during their childhood.

"It's not every day a Goddess and Guardian Angels appear to me not only in my dreams but when I'm supposed to be awake!"

Brigid shrugged and rolled her eyes once again, not the least bit ruffled by Quinn's outburst. "Newbie."

Quinn stared at her. "Newbie? This happens to you often, does it? Why didn't you tell me?"

"It's not something you go broadcasting to the world. People already think I'm a bit odd. If I told them I see spirits and angels, even our wacky family would be steering clear of me. Besides, you've been preoccupied lately."

Daniel took that as his cue to change the subject. "Brig is going to take care of things here while you're away at the Island."

Brigid's silver eyes twinkled. "That's right. The sooner you show me what you need for me to do around here, the quicker you'll be back in Jake's arms."

"You know about him, too?"

"I've known about him for a while, just not his name until last night. Besides, you talk in your sleep, girlie!" Brigid winked. "Go on. Get a pen so you can make me one of those lists you're so fond of drawing up." She watched as Quinn scurried out of the room and out of earshot. "She's got more than one hottie vying for her heart, Danny."

"I know. She'll have to go through hell and back to be with Jake." He knew he could trust the information with Brigid. The Goddess had given her special permission to help out. Normally, the angels had to alter the memories of people who came in contact with them, but not in this case. As a medium and priestess, Brigid would keep all that went on now to herself.

"We have to have faith that it will work out as planned. This is the only way to get all of these lives on the right path, but sometimes I feel like we're all pawns in a game between The Three. I know that sounds trite, but I don't understand why humans have to go through so much hell to get the happily ever after that's promised."

Daniel smiled. "I agree with you, but Fate has shown Michael and me more than just a glimpse into the future paths. Trust me. You've got a hunk waiting in the wings, too." He winked and laughed at the scowl that crossed her face.

Brigid smacked him on his arm. "Oh, you just knock it off! I'm perfectly happy with my life right now. Stop trying to be the matchmaker. I swear, if your ma and Randi had their way, I'd be married with a brood of babes in diapers." She grimaced, and some of the color drained from her face. "Not how I've envisioned my life going right now. Thank you very much!"

Quinn came back into the room with a stack of mail and a notebook. "Just what *have* you seen in those visions of yours?"

Brigid only smiled and shook her head. "Oh, that's a no-brainer. I'll be hanging out here taking care of you while you get all hot and heavy with your new stud muffin."

Quinn smiled and flopped down on the bed. "Brigid, he's so fucking hot! I can't keep my hands off of him." She sighed. "And the things he does to me—"

Daniel closed his eyes and covered his ears. "Stop! It's bad enough that I have to get flashes of the two of you in my head now, I don't need to hear the play-by-play!" Both women laughed hard. "How about you finish your list so we can get you back to him? He'll be waking up soon, and I'm sure you're gonna want to be there for that."

CHAPTER 19

"Merry Christmas, Jake. I don't know if you can hear me in there, but if you can, please come back. Your family has been here every day, waiting for your miracle." Kathy's eyes filled with tears, a rather common occurrence when she was alone with her patient. The guilt overwhelmed her at times, but she promised Michael she would keep working on that. She didn't want to have anything getting in the way of Jacob's recovery, and that included any bad vibes from her. "I'm so sorry for my part in this. I wish there was another way for you to get a new lease on life, but as your brother is fond of saying, you play the cards you're dealt with and make the best out of it. Sometimes the house is on your side. Personally, I think he's picked up too much of the Vegas lingo, but it does have a nice ring to it."

Michael slowly materialized next to Jacob's bed. Kathy had adjusted to the angel's sudden appearances and had managed to keep composed so as not to freak out his family. Katrina, on the other hand, knew right off. She would only wink and smile if the others were around. No need for that now. Just a few hours before, Kathy sent all the Hartleys back to the hotel with orders to try to get some sleep.

At the moment, only Kathy remained in the room. "He's been quite active today, Sarge. Dr. Evans is very happy with his test results, and his last surgery went well. He has a lot of metal in that leg and the opposite arm, but the repairs are sound. It's now up to him."

"Well then, this is as good a time as any to give him a little nudge. Jake's refusing to allow his mind and spirit to come back here because he's afraid he'll lose his chance to be with Quinn. Do you think you're up to giving me a hand?"

She decided it best to not question why but go with whatever would be asked of her. "What do you need me to do?"

"You're to be the only person he's going to see tonight. Just tell him the truth about what his body is going through. You're very good at telling patients what they need to hear and not scaring them. Jacob needs your skills now more than ever if he's to understand the long road he has ahead of him."

She trembled and tried to force the lump that had formed in her throat back down toward the pit of her stomach. "He's going to wake up? Shouldn't the rest of your family be here?" Kathy backed away from the bed and reached for the phone.

Michael shook his head. "Not this time. He won't be awake for very long, just enough to see that he's able to go between the worlds and find the strength to leave his soul mate." Michael laid his hands on his son's head and chest and smiled at the nurse. "Come on, what do you say? Give an old angel a hand?"

"Okay, I'll help however I can even though I don't understand any of it." She placed her hands-on Jacob's body, mirroring Michael's. A surge of heat passed through her from Jacob's body.

"You don't have to understand. Just have faith in your heart all will be as it should." Michael closed his eyes, and Kathy felt another surge of energy through Jacob and into her own hands and arms. She held her breath as a trembling began in her patient. A soft light surrounded all three of them. Kathy's mind remained on high alert, watching for any signs of trouble. She was prepared to intervene if needed, and she was grateful for her extensive medical training and ability to anticipate the needs of her patients.

Jacob's body lifted inches off the bed as the vibration grew stronger. He didn't appear to be having a seizure, but *something* was happening. As she watched in awe, the bruises on his face faded to pale purple and then yellow. The swelling of his eyelids diminished, and they fluttered as if he was in an active dream. His lips quivered around the endotracheal tube keeping his airway open while he remained unconscious.

With a sudden snap, his eyes opened, staring straight up at the ceiling. His breathing quickened and fought against the respirator. Struggling with the tube now, Jacob huffed, trying to cough it out. He blinked several times and turned to look into Kathy's eyes. He pointed to the tube and shook his head slowly, all the while imploring her with his eyes to explain what was happening.

"It's keeping your airway open while you recover."

He made a sharp pulling motion with his hand, never taking his eyes away from Kathy's, his confusion replaced with determination. He wanted the tube out and right now.

Kathy nodded and patted his bandaged hand closest to her. "Dr. Evans gave orders if you were awake and lucid we could pull it out for you." She looked to Michael for reassurance.

He smiled and gave her a quick nod. "Go ahead and remove that thing. He won't be needing it anymore. Merry Christmas, Jakey."

Kathy leaned forward and removed the tape securing the endotracheal tube in place to Jacob's face. "I want you to take a deep breath and, when I tell you, let it out and start coughing. Hard." She positioned herself so she had better access to the respirator. "Ready?" Jacob nodded.

"Inhale deeply and hold it." Kathy shut off the respirator, the oxygen supply attached to it, and then placed her fingers firmly around the tube. "Exhale and cough." She pulled the tube as Jacob expelled it from his body.

He swallowed hard a few times and then the coughing started up again. She handed him a cup of water with a straw. He took a few long pulls from it and dropped his head back onto the pillows. Jacob filled his lungs and slowly exhaled. He closed his eyes and tried to sit up. Kathy adjusted his bed so he could still be comfortable in the pillows but in a sitting position. His eyes widened as he took in all the wires, tubes, and IV lines attached to his body.

"How does it feel to be back?" Michael held his son's hand with both of his own.

Jacob licked his lips several times before trying to speak. All that would come out of him was a hoarse whisper. "Quinn?"

"She's making her own trip back here, but she'll be there waiting for you when you return. Daniel's with her now helping her get things in order so she can be back with you. I promise, both of you will be together shortly."

Kathy's mind reeled. "What do you mean? Go back? I thought your goal was to get him to come back here and live again?"

Jacob's eyes filled with tears. "Quinn?"

Michael patted his shoulder. "It's okay. You still have time together. We needed to bring you back to show you it can be done. Both of you have to return here to the real world soon enough, but if you didn't make some progress here, Lady Fate felt a some would lose faith of you ever returning."

Jacob wiped the tears from his face. "Eric?" His voice sounded stronger but hoarse.

The angel nodded. "Maredyth has all the faith in the world, but Eric's has been waning. Your mother trusts what will happen is meant to be, and she knows I'm here with you through it all. She's put your life in the hands of Fate and Yeshua. Eric has been struggling with seeing you like this with all these machines. If you didn't show him signs soon, he was going to discuss pulling the plug."

Jacob nodded and smiled slightly. "We had a pact. Neither one of us wanted to be hooked up to machines if there was no hope."

"I know you boys had a hell of a time seeing what I went through with my heart attack and stroke. What you need to understand is that your situation is very different. You have to believe in Fate and Yeshua and their plans for your future. You and Quinn have always been destined to be together."

He nodded and squeezed his father's hand. "How can I not have faith now? I've got you showing me the way." Jacob turned and reached for Kathy's hand with the arm that was in the cast. "Thank you."

"For what?" Kathy wanted to hear more about Jacob's destiny with Quinn and what they were doing on the Island. From what she'd heard so far, it sounded like a wonderful place.

"Thank you for, well, for being you."

Kathy hung her head. "I helped to put you here."

"No, you didn't, Kathy. I know you've heard this a few times already but listen to me. Deep down, I knew Julia was never faithful to me, but I chose to ignore it. You did *not* force me to get on the motorcycle, and you sure as hell didn't cause me to drive like an idiot in the rain. This was my fault, not yours." He squeezed her hand tighter. "Keep helping Eric so he understands what's happening. Help him believe in the miracles you get to see every day. Tell him I found mine."

Michael smiled at both of them. "Speaking of that, are you ready to go back to Quinn?"

"How long do we have?" Jacob's eyes sparkled when his father mentioned Quinn's name. Kathy had never seen that look on his face when he talked about Julia, not ever. She thought this had to be what it looked like when someone was head over heels in love, and the look suited him perfectly. She looked at Michael, eager to find out herself how much longer Jacob would be able to stay with Quinn.

"Stop worrying so much about how long and just enjoy the time you do have together." Michael knew his son was only concerned they wouldn't have enough time together and would be ripped apart before they were ready. He gripped Jacob's shoulder tight. "Son, you'll have long enough to complete your bond. Nothing and no one will keep you apart once you find each other again. You have my promise."

"And mine as well." All eyes turned to the foot of Jacob's bed. There stood Lady Fate, hair cascading down her back, a dark-purple gown draped elegantly over her curves. "You both will have to face some challenges in your lives before you can be completely reunited heart and soul. You will have your happily ever after together because of the choice you've both made now. Your path before you is now set. It's time, Jake. Quinn will be back from her journey and waking up soon. We don't want her to discover that you're taking your time returning, now, do we?"

Jacob laughed. "No, ma'am."

"Take your son back to the Island, Michael. I wish to have a few moments alone with Kathy if you don't mind."

"Merry Christmas, Kathy." He squeezed her hand one more time. "See you again soon." Jacob winked as he settled back onto his pillows and closed his eyes. Within moments, his breathing slowed to that of someone in a deep sleep. Michael waved as he faded from the room. Kathy waved back, wishing she was going with them.

"It's not your time yet either, child." The Goddess's melodic voice filled her head, and Kathy hung her head again. "No, Jacob spoke the truth. No blame lies at your feet. You are destined for great things in this lifetime and especially here at this hospital. I hear they are looking for a new person to run the ER."

"Dr. Carlos has that position—"

"No longer. He was forced to resign. You were not the only one he's taken advantage of over the years. With him gone, you no longer have his threats hanging over your head."

"Why me?" Kathy busied herself setting up the nasal oxygen tubing for Jacob in case it was needed, adjusting his pillows, and straightening his blankets.

"Look at you! Your first concern is always for your patients. At the expense of your own career, you saved Jacob from his chaotic life with Julia. He would have continued to be with her and let her change him. That was not acceptable to Us. Their time together was over, and you helped move him toward the path We chose for him long ago."

"All of this is so confusing. I was brought up to believe in God and to have faith that there's a reason for everything, but I guess I've developed a thick skin over the years. Seeing people go through the worst things imaginable can derail one's faith in a higher power or even in themselves. But after meeting angels and witnessing Jake heal right in front of my eyes, I *am* starting to believe again." Kathy frowned slightly. "What I don't understand is where do you fit in all of this? I went to Catholic school, and I don't recall learning about you."

Fate's laughter filled the room and made Kathy smile. "Oh yes, the Trinity. Well, part of that story is true, but as centuries pass, the stories become more fable than truth when left to humans to tell the tales. There *are* three of Us, just not equals. Yeshua, or as Daniel and Michael call him, the Big Guy, is the Master Creator. As the Goddess Fate, I am in charge of Destiny and ensuring each life path continues as it should. Then there is Lucius. He's the God of Trial and Tribulation, in charge of testing all of Our creations to find their true selves. Without the balance of The Three, all would be chaos, which Lucius has been in the middle of around here as of late."

Kathy looked down at Jacob. "It seems he's had more than his fair share of Lucius's trials and tribulations. I think he could use a break."

"We agree. That's why he's able to be with Quinn now. Believe it or not, Lucius agreed. He's really not all that bad you know. His is a thankless job, and there are times even I forget that." Fate smiled warmly. "Of course, I won't admit that very often in front of him."

Kathy laughed. She knew all about sibling rivalry, being the youngest of five. She didn't have the close relationship with her family that Jacob had with his, and now after the fiasco with Mario, she had never felt more alone in the world. Her heart cried out, needing to know if there was any hope for her.

"Is Jake really with his soul mate? I mean, do they exist?"

"They most certainly do exist. There is one for everyone even if they don't recognize it at first. Jacob and Quinn have been bound to each other through many lifetimes. They are two made from one. It's why they're so drawn to each other time after time."

"He deserves to be happy. He's such a kind-hearted person."

"As are you. Trust your heart, little one. It will never steer you wrong. The path before you is now clear. It's time to move forward." The Lady blew her a kiss and faded back into the wall. "One more thing, your soul mate is out there searching for you. Keep your eyes and heart open. You are the beacon that will bring him home to you."

Kathy's heart fluttered wildly. Angels and Goddesses appeared to her on a regular basis now, all because of one man. She picked up and squeezed Jacob's hand again. "Thank you for coming into my life now, Jacob Hartley. Thanks to you, I've found myself and my faith once again."

CHAPTER 20

Jacob's eyes opened and adjusted to the dim light of the bedroom. The scent of the salty ocean air filled his nose. He was back! He rolled over to find the space in the bed next to him empty. "Quinn?"

The curtains in front of the patio doors parted. "I'm outside waiting for the sun to come up. Care to join me?"

"Is that coffee I smell?" He tossed back the covers and grabbed the robe Quinn had laid out for him at the end of the bed. Like her, he found the taste of the coffee and all the food on the Island hard to resist. Everything was filled with such flavor. He would miss all of it when they had to go back.

"I just finished brewing a whole pot. We still have blueberry muffins left over from yesterday if you're hungry."

"The coffee is calling to me now, but a muffin would be great in a bit." Quinn handed him a large mug of the steaming brew as he took the seat next to her.

"Merry Christmas, baby doll."

"I love it when you call me that." She leaned over and kissed him. "Merry Christmas to you, too."

"Do you know what would make this day even better?"

Quinn shook her head. "What?"

He tugged on both of her hands, pulling her out of her chair and onto his lap. "Having you right here in my arms." He pulled her tight to his body as she laid her head on his shoulder. Jacob kissed her forehead and took a deep breath, taking in her sweet and spicy scent. "It's only been three days since my accident, but I thought we'd been here much longer."

"Daniel said time moves differently here. Sometimes it's faster and sometimes it's slower than in the real world. I kept asking him how much longer we had together. Finally, he just got fed up with it and told me to quit worrying about it and enjoy every moment." Quinn chuckled. "He would always get so frustrated when I quizzed him repeatedly about anything. He never stopped trying to get me to just go with it and enjoy myself."

"And how's that going for you?" Jacob knew what she meant. He was having the same problem. Maybe it was time to just accept it all, stop asking so many questions and just enjoy the time they had together.

"That's why I was out here when you woke up. I made a promise to myself I would enjoy every minute here and experience all there is, starting with the sunrise. I understand now why Danny and Michael haven't told us exactly how long we are able to stay here. Dwelling on saying goodbye to you, even for just a little while, will eat me up inside. If this turns out to be our last day together, I want to spend every single moment with you. That way, no matter how or when I find myself back in my own room in Michigan, I'll have no regrets." Her voice was a little muffled against his chest, but he could tell she was fighting back tears.

He pulled her chin up so she had to look in his eyes. "We'll have to make the most of whatever time we have left here in this paradise. It may be a few weeks or just a few more days. However long, I want every minute with you."

Her arms wrapped around his neck as their lips touched again, gently at first and then with more urgency, their tongues slipping and sliding over each other. Her body melted into his, offering herself to him and at the same time staking her claim on his heart.

"Keep kissing me like that and we'll miss the sunrise you got me out of bed to witness."

She giggled and settled back in his arms. "Don't think you can distract me for too long. As soon as that sunrise is over, you are mine, Hartley."

He laughed and squeezed her tight. "I think the show is about to start." Together they watched the sky as it changed from the dark of night to the dawn of a new day. The purples and crimsons morphed into oranges and yellows. The colors reflected off the water, creating a burst of vibrant images before their eyes. "Beautiful."

He was no longer looking at the brilliant display in the sky but at Quinn. His heart felt full for the very first time in his life. This was what it was like to be with the one person who completed him. No more doubts filled his mind. "I love you. I think I've loved you through several lifetimes, but something about right here and now is different."

She smiled and placed her hand on his stubbly cheek. "I love you, too. Maybe knowing and believing that we'll find each other when we go back is making it so much easier to let go here. At first, I didn't believe we weren't going to be torn apart again, but this sunrise? It's the sign I was looking for. Fate said Yeshua would give us a sign. That's it."

"Lady Fate promised me we would be together this time, too. I think you're right. That's the perfect way to signal to us they didn't forget."

"Was that the first time you've ever seen Fate? I mean, have you ever wondered if The Three really existed?"

"My mother always prayed to them. As a kid, I believed, but as I grew up, I lost my way. Now because of you, your brother and my pop, I'm believing again."

"I've prayed to the Goddess for years and have seen her in my dreams, but I think a small part of me didn't believe completely in The Three. Everything's changed and to have this visit with her now, well, it was all surreal."

Jacob kissed her neck. "Being here with *you* is surreal, but I'm not going to argue with it."

"Me either."

He stood up with Quinn still wrapped in his arms. "Well, I've got an idea of how I want to pledge my love for you. Are you game?"

Jacob nibbled on her neck, eliciting a sigh. "I'll take that as a yes."

CHAPTER 21

Quinn had never felt safer or more secure than in Jacob's arms. All of her remaining doubts and fears of losing him vanished as his hungry mouth devoured hers. She surrendered herself completely to him. It no longer mattered how long they had together, as long as they could be in each other's arms now.

Jacob nibbled on her neck as he carried her back to the bed they shared the night before. Standing her at the foot of it, he untied her robe and let it slip from her body, trailing kisses along her shoulder. She reached between them to open his robe, tracing her fingertips along his well-muscled abs. She molded her body to his, feeling their hearts beat in sync with each other.

Her hands slid up his arms and around his neck as he eased her back onto the bed, covering her body completely with his own. Jacob's muscles rippled under her fingertips, the heat of his flesh on hers sending jolts of electricity right to her very core. Her breath caught in her chest momentarily as their eyes locked. She fell deeper into the blue orbs with every beat of her heart. "I love you, Jake. Promise me you won't give up looking for me after we go back."

His eyes filled with tears. "Never. No matter what happens, I'll fight for you, Quinn. Don't give up on me. I love you with all that I am and all that I hope to be." His right knee eased between hers. Quinn slid her left leg up to hook over his hip. Her fingers combed through his long hair while their tongues slowly slipped over each other, giving, taking, teasing, and surrendering.

They rolled over, Jake pulling Quinn so she was now on top, her legs straddling his hips. Her full breasts ached with the need to be suckled. Sitting up, she offered them to him. He took one nipple and then the other into his mouth, sucking hard one moment, flicking them rapidly with his tongue the next. Quinn moaned as his teeth grazed each sensitive tip. Her body shuddered, releasing more hot cum from her pussy. She pushed him back on the bed, pinning his arms over his head. "Not so fast. It's my turn."

Quinn eased herself down Jacob's body, licking, kissing, and tasting his salty, deeply tanned skin. She settled between his legs, nuzzled his inner thighs and planted kisses along his skin. She balanced his balls in her hands, kneading them while tracing the underside of his swollen cock with the flat portion of her tongue.

Jacob gasped as she wrapped her other hand around his shaft, slowly stroking up and down. "Don't stop, baby. It feels unbelievable."

Quinn held his sultry gaze as she licked the velvety tip of his cock with the point of her tongue, lapping up the pre-cum quickly. "You *taste* unbelievable!" She smiled slowly before she took him into her mouth, swirling her tongue around it rapidly before plunging down the shaft. Relaxing her throat, she took as much of him in as she could and then pulled him out with an audible pop. Jacob jumped and groaned as she took him deep into her mouth again, wrapping her hand snuggly around the base, squeezing a little as she worked to bring him to the edge.

Jacob sat up and reached for her. "I need you now, Quinn." He eased her up his legs and held her in position as the tip of his dick teased her wet, velvety slit. Her head tilted back as she lowered herself, embedding him deep inside her pussy, filling and stretching it to accommodate all of him. She held still and allowed the sensation of being connected to him wash over her. Her mind wanted to savor the feeling, but her body had other plans. Her hips ground into him, trying to pull him in deeper if that was even possible.

His hands moved up to her waist, keeping her steady as she continued to control the pace of their lovemaking. Quinn had never felt more powerful or out of control at the same time. She knew she held Jacob's heart and soul in her hands, but he held hers as well. Both had the power to complete the other or to destroy them both. That knowledge only fanned the flames of the love she felt for him. She was both fascinated and frightened by the depth of her emotions for him, but there was no way in hell she could turn back now even if the thought crossed her mind.

* * * *

Jacob's heart fluttered wildly out of fear. Fear of letting go to fall head over heels in love with Quinn and of losing her and the love she gave to him so freely. No one had ever pushed through all of the walls around his heart as quickly as she had. Quinn had looked deep into his soul and still embraced him, offering her love in return. That alone made him feel powerful and yet vulnerable at the same time. Could Fate really be on their side in all of this, or would they be torn apart by forces yet unknown?

He pushed those thoughts to the back of his mind as Quinn's arms wrapped tightly around his neck. He grabbed her ass and squeezed hard while she plunged repeatedly up and down on his cock, coating them both in her juices. Her body shook violently as another orgasm whipped through her, merely seconds after the last one. "Don't let me go, Jake. Please don't let me go!"

"Never." Jacob held her tight and flipped her on her back. Keeping her legs wrapped around his hips, he plunged into her hard and fast. Her nails raked down his back, urging him to pound into her. "You're mine, now and forever." Her pussy clenched his cock hard, pulling him deep inside, bringing him to the edge with her.

"Now and forever." Quinn gazed deeply into his eyes as they came together one last time.

CHAPTER 22

Daniel watched his sister run through the waves with Jacob. He didn't remember seeing her that happy in a hell of a long time. She had been there with Jacob for what seemed like several weeks to them but was actually less than two in the real world. Michael was anxious to convince his son to go back. If he waited much longer, the choice would be made for him and he might not like the outcome. "We need to tell them. They won't go back otherwise."

"Danny, you know very well we can't tell them exactly when they'll find each other again. They still have to go through some other trials left ahead of them. Even if we nudge and nudge, their free will is what'll decide the how and the when. And you do realize we'll have to block their memories of this place, at least for a while? When they go back, Jake and Quinn won't remember their time here until they're reunited again in the earth realm."

"I don't want her to go through any more pain. There's a hell of a lot of that ahead of her. Quinn's opened up to Jake here. If we block them from remembering their time together, we'll take away all the progress she's made. She'll go back to burying everything again and be in worse shape than she was before she came to the Island. Quinn still hasn't completely worked through her feelings about my death, and much too soon after she has to leave Jake and go back, her world will be turned upside down yet again. Our entire family will suffer right along with her when my dad finds out about the non-Hodgkin's lymphoma. Less than a year later he'll be gone, and there's nothing I can do to ease anyone's pain here. I feel so helpless!" Daniel flung a rock far out into the ocean.

"We'll be here for all of them, Danny. It's what we do. As for Jake and Quinn..." Michael appeared deep in thought for a moment, and then his face lit up. "I got it. We tell them just enough truth to get them to leave here. Then it's up to them to choose their own paths. When they meet again, their connection will be so strong, they'll be able to use it to come back to the Island together when they need each other the most. There're just too many variables to play out yet, but I tell you what. Even though we can't give them an exact *date* when they'll be reunited, we can tell them where."

Daniel raised one eyebrow. "Vegas?"

Michael nodded slowly. "That city will be a huge part of both of their lives from this point on. Why wouldn't it be the place where they find each other again?"

"Las Vegas sounds great to me. I always wanted to live there before..." Daniel sighed. Sometimes being this close to his family and not able to experience life with them brought the old fear back to his mind. Was he really cut out to be a Guardian? "Does this stuff get any easier?"

"Yes and no. Until they paired me up with you, I didn't have a clue how to get through this stuff, let alone watch over my own family. You were right before. They wouldn't have put us in charge of all of these couples if they didn't think we could do it."

Both angels started down the beach toward their loved ones. "Please tell me Jake goes for the dueling dragons tattoo. It would look fantastic covering his back."

Michael laughed hard. "Let's just get them both back safely before we go through with your plan to start covering them both in ink, shall we?"

"Okay, I'll let it go for now, but only because I've been thinking a lot about our other charges lately. Overall, everyone is moving in the right direction, but I think we're going to have to do some major nudging with one particular person."

"Ah, you think Derek will be hard to convince to keep the faith?"

"He's been through a lot of shuffling through foster homes. It may take some doing to get him to trust again."

"Then I think the two of us are right for the job. Between both of our families, Derek will find exactly what he's been missing. All he needs is just a bit of inspiration."

Daniel nodded. "He's my special project this time around. Quinn's going to need him to get through Dad's cancer and death."

Michael nodded. "He will take good care of her just as you would. Lady Fate thought Derek would interest you, being a musician and an artist no less."

"And covered in tattoos, too. Don't forget the ink!"

The elder angel laughed again and placed his hand on Daniel's shoulder. "How could we ever forget about the ink?"

* * * *

Quinn slipped out of Jacob's grasp and dashed up the beach toward his bungalow. Scratch that, *their* bungalow. Instead of switching lodging every few days as they had been, they decided a week ago to pick one place and make it special, hoping to make lasting memories of every moment together in the tropical paradise. The hot tub on the deck of Jacob's quarters was a little bigger than the other, so for Quinn, it was an easy choice. Jacob, on the other hand, preferred her kitchen and grill area. She wasn't buying that one for a second though. She knew he loved her bungalow more because she tended to take over the cooking while they stayed there. Not that she minded it at all. She loved to cook, but Jacob was quite the grill master himself and Quinn enjoyed it when he kicked her out of the kitchen from time to time.

To get him to agree to the move, Quinn had to accept the challenge to outrun him back to their new Island home, and he got to choose when the race would take place. Of course, she accepted the challenge before she found out the stipulations. Jacob held off telling her what those were right up to an hour ago, probably hoping he would throw her off her A game if she didn't know what to expect. Although he didn't succeed in doing that, Jacob did surprise her with the details of the competition itself.

The loser of the race had to do all the cooking and cleanup. That part alone sealed the deal for her. She hated to be stuck with the cleanup duties. Of course, Jacob wasn't going to make it easy. He stipulated they had to run in and out of the waves as they tried to make it down the shore. Running in dry sand was hard enough but slipping and sliding in the wet stuff was a tad more difficult. Several times he had her nearly tackled in the surf, but she managed to slip out of his arms. Finally, she could take no more. She was laughing and dodging him more than running. They weren't making any forward progress at all, which Quinn realized was exactly the plan from the beginning. She couldn't keep going any further and decided enough was enough.

Jacob wrapped his arms around her and sunk down into the waves, pulling her onto his lap and laughing along with her. "Good God, woman! I didn't think you'd ever tire out. I was about to give in myself. What do you say we share the cooking and cleanup?" He closed his eyes and rested his forehead against hers, both of them still trying to bring their breathing back to normal. "Hell, if you promise we don't have to run through the water like that again, I'll do the dishes every single time."

Quinn laughed harder and wrapped her arms around his neck. "It was your idea to race like that."

"Well, I didn't think you'd take me up on it." He smiled, and Quinn felt breathless once again. "But now that you've finally come to your senses and let me catch you, how about we get out of these wet bathing suits and soak in that hot tub you're so fond of?"

She kissed him softly and shook her head. "Sorry, honey. We're not alone. I could be wrong, but it looks to me like we've got some angelic company."

Jacob stood up with her still wrapped tightly around his body and turned his eyes up toward the bungalow. Quinn felt her lover's heart pound, matching the rhythm of her own. He held her tighter, crushing her bikini-covered breasts against his bare chest. "Do you think they've come to tell us our time's up?"

His arms tightened around her, and she sensed his rising panic. Oddly enough, she wasn't afraid. "Babe, it's okay. Whatever they have to say to us now, it's going to be okay."

"I know we agreed we would go back when they came for us but I'm not ready to let you go. I need just a little more time." His voice was barely above a whisper, and Quinn barely heard him over the sound of the waves.

She pulled back and placed her hands on either side of his face, gazing deep into his eyes. "I know, but we chose our paths and now we have to move forward." Quinn waved to Daniel and Michael and kissed him again. "We'll be together again before we know it."

Jacob helped Quinn out of the surf, holding her hand tightly as they walked up the beach together. "It looks like they're smiling. Has to be a good sign, right?"

She smiled and rested her head against his upper arm. "How about we ask them?"

Her brother and Jacob's father made themselves right at home, sitting in the cushioned chairs on the deck near the hot tub. Daniel's eyes met hers and he smiled broadly. "Ask us what?"

"What brings the two of you here today?" Jacob's voice faltered as he stared at his father, waiting for an answer. Quinn hoped he wasn't right and they weren't there to take them back. But if it was time, then that was that. She wanted the future promised to them and the only way to get that was to leave their safe haven and each other when their time together there was at an end.

Michael gestured to the empty seats opposite the two of them. "Why don't you both get comfortable and we can get down to it?"

"Pop, if you're here to take us back now, just come out and say the words. Please don't drag it out any longer than it has to be."

The angels quickly glanced at each other and turned back to the couple. "Son, we're not here to separate you. It's not time for you to go back yet."

Quinn finally found her voice again. "Why are you here then?"

"Danny and I thought the two of you would like to hear about what you have to look forward to once you go back. Some of it's not very pretty, but everything leads you back to each other."

Jacob exhaled and relaxed his grip on Quinn's hand long enough to help her get seated in the chair next to her brother. "I'm guessing I've got a lot of rehab ahead of me."

Michael nodded gravely. "That you do. You're going to have to fight each and every day to get back your physical abilities. That's actually the easiest part. It's going to take a hell of a lot longer for your heart and mind to heal."

Quinn squeezed Jacob's hand tighter. "I'll do what I can to help with that."

Her brother smiled. "You are the reason he'll be able to heal. Without your love, he would remain lost and broken. The memories of the time you've spent together will be with you always but will be locked away in your mind for a little while until the time is right for your reunion."

"Is it because there are still people who we have to meet and learn lessons from before we can be together again?" Quinn wanted to ask how long it would be before she would be with Jacob, but she knew the Guardians couldn't tell them the answer to that. She had to admit to herself it was probably best they didn't know. For now, it was enough to know The Three would fulfill their promise to them and let them be together.

Daniel nodded. "When you find each other again, Jacob's healing will be complete. You, on the other hand, have some difficult choices to make with your career and personal life. Until you're reunited with Jake, you will have someone to stand by you through it all."

* * * *

Jacob's jaw dropped. "You can't be serious? She's already been through too much losing you. It's hard enough that we're going to be separated again, does she really have to go through more pain?"

Daniel's eyes glistened. "There are some things we just can't change no matter how hard we want to do so. We can't always be there to help the two of you get through what still lies ahead, but you will have our families and some new friends. One, in particular, will befriend you both in Las Vegas. He is someone you both will be drawn to because of his passion for music and artwork."

"Is that where we find each other again? Vegas?" Jacob looked at Quinn and smiled. "My brother Eric loves the place. I had thought about following him out there until—"

"Until Julia. You don't have to worry about her anymore. She's most definitely in your past. Quinn is your present and future." Michael put his hand on his son's shoulder, squeezing it gently. "You don't have to be afraid, son."

Quinn turned to her brother. "Who's this special friend we'll meet in Vegas? Do I already know him?

"No, but you will meet him very soon." Daniel smiled. "You'll take to each other right off, and before you get your panties in a bunch, Jake, relax. He's in no way competition. Derek is more like a brother. He'll be able to take care of you and the family in ways I can't any longer. Honestly, I would've loved to have a big brother like him growing up. No offense."

Quinn laughed. "None taken." She reached for Daniel's hand and held it, while Jacob held his father's. The four of them sat a moment in the circle before the silence was broken by Michael clearing his throat.

"I know seeing us here tonight took the wind out of both of you, but we just wanted to give you one more pep talk. Don't be afraid to go back. You will find each other, and once you do, the sparks will fly. There will be no denying the two of you belong together. Even those around you will see from the very first time you meet in Vegas that you belong with each other."

"I'm not afraid. I told Fate I choose Jacob and everything that goes along with that decision. My heart won't let me go down any other path."

Jacob nodded. "I guess the old fears of failure were nagging at the back of my mind, but I'm not afraid of the future anymore knowing Quinn will be by my side."

"That settles it then. Danny and I will leave the two of you alone to enjoy the rest of your evening together."

"One more thing." Daniel pulled Quinn close to stare deep into her eyes. "Promise me once again you will live your life to the fullest. Don't give up, not ever again. Promise?"

Quinn smiled. "I'll do better than that." She held up her right hand with her little finger extended. "Pinky swear."

Daniel smiled and hooked her pinky with his. "Pinky swear." He turned to Jacob one more time and nodded. "Take care of her, brotha. You know I'll be watching." He winked and let Quinn settle back into Jacob's arms.

"I will. She's my heart and soul." He kissed her forehead. "Thank you both for bringing us together and giving me a reason to live again."

Michael hugged his son. "You've always had it in you, Jakey. We just helped bring it out. Besides, Lady Fate wasn't about to give up on either one of you. It was only a matter of time until you came around." He reached for Quinn and held her in a bear hug. "You are his guiding light, and I'm so happy we were able to bring you together now."

"Me, too."

The Guardians turned and walked toward the beach. They faded slowly with each step until they vanished into the crashing waves. Jacob rubbed Quinn's back as they watched the tide come in. "I'm not afraid anymore, baby doll. If the next sunrise we see isn't here in this paradise, I know it won't be long before we're together again."

She smiled and kissed him. "Come on. Let's get out of these bathing suits and into that hot tub. I think we have another bottle of that wine you love so much. How about we have a glass or two of that while we watch another sunset?"

His heart beat a bit faster. She felt it, too. Their new life together was about to begin.

CHAPTER 23

"You both handled that very well. You told them what they needed to know in order to reassure them they had chosen wisely to leave each other now and ensure their happily ever after back in the Earth Realm. We couldn't have chosen anyone better to watch over Jake and Quinn." The Goddess Fate watched the couple asleep, wrapped in each other's arms. "Now it's time for them to leave here."

Daniel nodded. "It's nearly midnight on New Year's Eve. Both Brigid and Kathy are expecting them to wake up any time now." He was relieved they were able to give them the one last night together happy without knowing for sure their time was up. Good-byes were never his strong suit and he hated to watch while others had to be separated for any length of time.

As soon as they fell into a deep sleep, Jake and Quinn's time on the Island began to fade to the recesses of their minds, keeping their memories safe until the day they would relive each and every one of them together. Because both of them chose to leave the Island to face the unknown challenges before them, their future was now set. They were finally on the path that would lead them back to each other.

"Don't worry, Daniel. Lucius has promised to let them remember all of their time here. Their memories are safely locked away until the time they're brought together once more."

"Steve's club Saints and Sinners will be the catalyst." Michael smiled. "Both will be drawn to Vegas year after year, but until they're in the club at the same time, neither will remember anything. The fateful night when their eyes lock on each other on the dance floor will set everything in motion. From that moment on, nothing and no one will be able to keep them apart for very long. They will face obstacles standing in their way, but the love they have for each other will win out in the end."

Fate raised her hands and sent two balls of pale green light to surround the couple, still sound asleep, completely oblivious to their three visitors. As the light grew brighter, Quinn and Jake slowly faded from view. "Soon they will awaken and begin their journey back to one another."

"I still feel guilty not telling them how long it will be before they find each other." Daniel hung his head a bit and closed his eyes, afraid the tears would fall again.

"As my brother reminded me, their time apart is but a blink of an eye. None of it will matter once they are together again. Besides, you didn't know yourself how long it would be before their reunion until only moments ago. Don't feel guilty for something you had no control over in the first place."

Daniel knew Fate was right. He still had a lot to learn if he was to continue to watch over his family and others. He was grateful to be paired with Michael, too. Together they made a pretty good team.

"Come on, Danny. We've got a few more folks to check on tonight before Jake and Quinn wake up."

"I hope two of those people happen to be Julia and Carmen." Fate's smile widened. "It appears a few more nudges are in order with those two, wouldn't you say?"

Daniel laughed. "We'll get right on that."

* * * *

Lucius's fingers flew over the laptop keyboard faster than the human eye could detect. As a god, he didn't have to use the fancy electronics to perform any of his tasks, but he was fascinated that the human brain could actually come up with the marvels. Of course, Yeshua loved to point out to him the humans had always been their finest creations because of their ability to change and adapt to whatever was thrown at them. Lucius would concede that *some* humans had that ability, but more often than not he found the rest of them sorely lacking. Those were the type who sat back and let others tell them what to do, say, or think. It was because of them Lucius rained so much adversity down on Earth. He wanted to find those few who actually deserved all the blessings available to them if they would only reach out for it.

With a few more clicks, he brought up those creations they were gathered to discuss. This time all were happy with the turn of events, especially Yeshua. Lucius wasn't sure what exactly had his eldest sibling the happiest. The fact that Jacob and Quinn were finally on their destined path with each other or that the three of them were actually smiling and laughing together for the first time in a few millennia.

Yeshua sat up straighter in his chair and positively beamed. "Your smile lights up the room, dear sister. It's been far too long since you've laughed during our gatherings. Is it all because of Jake and Quinn?"

"A great deal yes, but also the work of our Guardians. They've made wise choices in their dealings with humans. Through saving Jake and Quinn's bond, they've managed to renew the faith of so many." She waved her hand toward the screen and smiled even brighter. "Look at them! All the couples in question are on the correct paths now. We've even managed to pick up a few more along the way."

Lucius smiled as his brother's ice-blue eyes fell on him. "What are your thoughts, brother? Are they all moving forward as you wish?"

"With a little nudge here and there, they'll stay the course for the next ten years."

Fate's eyes widened. "Does it really have to be so long?"

"We've discussed this before. Ten years is but a blink of an eye. They'll make it through. I need them to test a few others along the way." Lucius tilted his head toward the screens. "These are not the only humans I have to deal with, as you know."

The Goddess turned toward Yeshua, pleading with her eyes to speak up and change things. It was hard not to give in to her when she did that, but both of them had an eternity to develop thick skins. The Eldest reached across the table at which they were seated to take her hand. "It is as it should be, Fate. We've intervened enough for now. It's time we trust them to continue their journey. The humans are not the only beings who have to have faith."

"I promise you I won't keep them apart longer than necessary." Lucius took her other hand and squeezed it tightly. "Jacob and Quinn have a beautiful life together very soon. Eventually, I'll even let them remember their time on the Island."

Fate continued to hold her brothers' hands and smiled once again. "Well, we've waited this long, what's a few more years when their reward will be magical?"

Yeshua chuckled and winked. "That's my girl. Let's see how our Guardians are making do with some of the others, shall we?"

Lucius picked up the remote and clicked a few buttons to focus in on one person. "Let's see how Julia's getting along now. I have to admit, I have a soft spot for her, too."

"Daniel wasn't sure he was the best choice as her Guardian, but as he watched her he understood why you asked for him specifically, Lucius."

"In spite of what you think of me at times, I do think those humans who fight to find their way deserve a second chance. Julia, Jake, Quinn, and the others have what it takes inside them to be truly happy. I just want them to stand their ground and stick up for themselves."

Fate laughed. "You got your wish with this bunch, no?"

"And then some." Lucius winked and turned his attention back to the flat screens covering the wall. "How about we fast-forward a bit and check in on them in, oh, let's say thirteen years from now?"

CHAPTER 24

February 13, Las Vegas, Present Day

Quinn rocked her son as he nursed. Even though the twins were now using bottles for most of their feedings, Quinn still enjoyed the one-on-one time with each child first thing in the morning and usually one more time before they went to sleep. She was a firm believer in nursing her children as long as she could, well up to the age of two. If the kids were old enough to ask for it, they were old enough not to be suckling at her breast.

Stephanie had been the first one awake and able to breastfeed first. She gurgled and cooed the entire time, and Quinn was surprised Danny slept through it all. More often than not, he would be the first up, but according to Brigid, he stayed up much later than his sister, not wanting to fall asleep and miss anything. Both babies loved spending time with the family, often missing naps to keep the fun rolling. Jacob didn't mind that one bit since it meant both tots would then sleep through the night.

Most of the time, he would help out with the morning routine, but today Jacob had to meet Eric bright and early. He did check in on them before he left and found them both sound asleep, snoring softly. Of course, he reminded her once again they inherited that particular trait from her!

Brigid slowly rocked Stephanie in the chair next to Quinn. "You know, I think Steph has Jake's deep-blue eyes and Danny has your ocean blue-green color. Just as it should be."

Quinn smiled. "Well, he is named after his uncle and grandpa. It seems fitting he has their eye color as well." She adjusted Danny to her shoulder when he finished nursing and continued to rock and burp him a bit. "I hope they didn't wear you out last night. I can really use some help keeping an eye on them when we visit Derek's shop this afternoon."

"Are you kidding? I'd love to help out with them. I haven't been able to see them as much as I've wanted over the last year. Oh, and you know as soon as your ma and sister get here, I'll be lucky to get any face time with them. That's why I took you up on your invitation to come out early. Plus, I can't wait to see Derek. I have an idea for a new tat I'd like to run by him."

"Oh, he'd love that! He's been dying to get you back in his chair for some time now. This afternoon is my turn though. I had him design one for my anniversary." Quinn pulled out a paper from her pocket and handed it to her cousin. It was a rough sketch of a tropical island at sunrise with the words "My Heart and Soul" at the top and "Always and Forever" at the bottom. "What do you think? This is just something he sketched while I threw ideas at him. You should see the color picture he drew up. It's beautiful and just what I want to have on my back. You know, in the left shoulder area?"

Brigid grinned broadly. "Perfect spot for it since you have the dragons covering your lower back." She looked at the picture one more time and handed it back to Quinn. "Is this the Island, the one you can travel to in your dreams?" Quinn nodded and returned the smile. "Have you remembered more of your time there?"

"It's all coming back now. Meeting with Jake's ex-girlfriend last night opened up the floodgates. The time we spent there thirteen years ago and again two years ago when we thought we lost each other forever all came rushing back as we talked about it. No wonder we experienced so many moments of déjà vu. It all happened."

"I wanted to tell you so many times, but I couldn't. You had to find your way back to each other without those memories. I knew you'd get there. You had Steve and Derek to help. They were the key for you and Jake then and for a few other people yet."

"What do you mean?" Quinn got up to start getting little Danny ready for the day. She winked and smiled. "Are you keeping secrets from me again?"

"Who me?" Brigid giggled, eliciting a similar sound from little Stephanie. "Oh, I think we have another Wiccan priestess in the making here. You can help me keep the secrets, huh, Stephie?"

"Spill it, Brig." Danny splashed in the little portable bathtub and laughed along with his sister. "Now don't you turn on me, too, little man!"

"Have you ever wondered why you had such a strong bond with Derek right from the moment you met?"

Quinn shook her head. "Not really. It just felt right with him straight away. The entire family, including you, took to him right from the start."

"There's a reason for that." Brigid bounced her little cousin on her knee as she continued. "And it just so happens to be why you've not had very many visitations from your brother since the Island."

"What are you saying? Derek and Danny are one and the same person now?" Quinn froze and stared at her purple-haired cousin.

"No. A *part* of Danny lives on in him though. That way he can always be with you and the rest of us. It's a gift from The Three, as were your bambinos."

"I knew it." Quinn's eyes glistened with tears. "I knew all along Derek was meant to be in our family, as sure as I was that Jake and I were meant to be together right from the moment I caught him watching me on that dance floor."

Brigid nodded and smiled. "It's all as it should be. Just so you know, there are more surprises to come in the days ahead."

"Must you always speak in riddles?" Quinn laughed and shook her head while she dressed her son.

"It's who I am, and you still love me." Brigid blew her a kiss, and immediately Stephanie tried to mimic her.

Quinn smiled and blew a kiss back to the baby, eliciting a volley of giggles and more kiss throwing from both tots. "Even though that part bugs me at times, I wouldn't want you any other way. How about I fix us something to eat before heading out to The Tattoo Parlor?"

"Ah, I knew there was a reason you're my favorite cousin!"

* * * *

"I admit I wasn't thrilled that you and Quinn agreed to meet with Julia, but after what you've told me, I can see it was time. Your wife was right." Eric slathered his hot pancakes with more whipped butter and covered them in syrup.

Jacob smiled. His brother's appetite never ceased to amaze him. Even as kids he could pile away the food. "She usually is right, but what specifically are you referring to?"

"Thirteen years is a hell of a long time to hold a grudge. When Steve said he wanted to have Julia come to Vegas and discuss more artwork for the club, I wanted no part of it. When she walked into the office yesterday, I couldn't help but notice the changes in her and decided to hear her out."

"And?" He knew it had to be hard for Eric to see her again after all this time.

"Well, first of all, she didn't look like the spoiled rich artist from LA. Julia still has that confidence about her, but it's not arrogance if you know what I mean."

Jacob nodded. "She's no longer all ready for the paparazzi."

"Exactly. She walked into the club with several sketch books with her as well as another portfolio filled with photos of her older stuff. You know, with all that happened, I forgot how truly talented she was and still is. Steve showed her around and told her what he had in mind and all the while she was busy sketching ideas as he talked."

"She never did that before. Julia would listen briefly to what a client wanted and then would go off and do whatever popped into her head, never caring what the client really wanted."

"Not this time. She took everything we mentioned during that meeting and came up with exactly what Steve had envisioned. She is one hell of an artist and it was those sketches she did on the fly that sold me."

"The dinner was a bit awkward at first for all of us, but by the end of the night, we managed to work through everything, too. We did get one shocker. Julia's had similar experiences on the Island."

Eric stopped chewing and his jaw dropped. "You're shitting me, right? I thought that place was just something only you and Quinn shared."

Jacob shook his head. "Apparently not. More of our time there comes back to us each day now. It's no longer just our dream world. It's becoming real."

"Do you think you can go back there again if you wanted to?" Eric pushed his now-empty plate to the side and started in on Jacob's marble rye toast. "You weren't going to eat this, were you?"

"Go ahead." Jacob chuckled. "I've been thinking about trying to go back. Quinn's been teaching me some dream walking techniques. I was hoping we could try to make the trip this evening after the twins are out for the night."

"What happens if you two make it there and the twins need you here?"

"Quinn's cousin's staying with us in the suite. She's agreed to keep an eye on all of us during the night just in case."

Eric smiled and raised his eyebrows up and down rapidly. "Just in case? You got a little sex-on-the-beach rendezvous planned?"

Jacob nearly spit his coffee across the table. "Jeez, Eric! You talk like that in front of your nieces and nephews?" He grabbed his brother's napkin and mopped up the coffee from the tabletop and his shirt.

"Of course not." Eric sat up straight in his chair, smile still plastered across his face. "But I know ever since the wonder twins were born you and Quinn have had little time alone with each other. How often do you have someone from both sides of the family show up to 'help' you guys out?"

"We seem to have a revolving door. Don't get me wrong. I loved having the help in the beginning while we were trying to figure out the feeding schedules and everything, but it would be nice to have a date night or two here and there. What better place than where we first found each other?"

"Is that why you decided to come out here a week before Quinn's veterinary conference?"

"It was Quinn's idea. She thought if we got the family together out here, we could celebrate the twins' first birthday and our anniversary all at one time with everyone in one place. With everyone vying to spend time with the kids, we could get a little alone time."

As more early risers filtered into the Studio Café, Eric signaled to their waitress for their check. "Don't worry. One way or another, I'll make sure the two of you get that downtime. If anyone deserves to get back to the Island, it's the two of you. Until then, how about you help me pick up Ma and Maredyth at the airport?"

"Perfect. I don't have to be over at Derek's until this afternoon." They strolled out onto the casino floor. It had been a few years since he'd been back, and he was surprised at how much he missed the place. Quinn had said the same to him last night. "We got some time to look at some properties nearby?"

Eric stopped in his tracks. "You thinking of moving back here?"

Jacob smiled and shrugged. "Let's just say I've gotta feeling and leave it at that."

"I hope you have more than just a feeling. You know as soon as word gets back to Steve, he'll start the ball rolling."

"Well, then let's just keep it between the two of us for now. If my hunch is correct, Quinn's going to want to be out here when they start building the new veterinary specialty center in Henderson."

"I never thought I'd see the day when I would be helping my big brother look for a house in Vegas of all places."

"This place is special to both of us. Why not here?"

The valet pulled up with Eric's Range Rover and tossed him the keys. "Hey, I'm not trying to talk you out of it. I think this is the perfect place for both of you. You forget, I witnessed your thunderstruck moment on that dance floor. If that happened to me, I'd be setting up house with my honey right here, too."

"Speaking of that, Jillian should arrive later this afternoon. You got plans to pick her up at the airport, too?"

Eric blushed and smiled slyly. "I've got something else planned for her arrival, and no, I'm not going to tell you. I don't need you and Maredyth harassing me about it and making me more nervous than I already am."

"Have it your way, but you know our sister. She will get it out of you before you've loaded up their luggage in the back of this monster."

"Don't remind me. Why don't you tell me more about your meeting with Julia and what you remembered about your time on the Island?"

"Nice! Turn the focus away from Jillian and back to me. Okay, I'll play your game."

CHAPTER 25

Quinn watched Brigid set up a play zone for the twins in the waiting area of The Tattoo Parlor and smiled. Within moments of their arrival, nearly all the tattoo artists dropped what they were doing in order to get a good look at the giggling babies. Not one of them believed it had been a year since they were born. Her children reached for each artist in turn, laughing and chattering in their own language to all the adults. It was a tad chaotic but enjoyable for everyone nonetheless. Little Danny, in particular, was fascinated by the tattoos covering his Uncle Derek's arms, his eyes wide as his little fingers touched each color. Derek told him the story behind each one he touched, eliciting more of the toddler oohs and aahs.

Now both were in the portable playpen crawling after their favorite toys and laughing at the funny faces Brigid did while she read from their favorite book. Well, it was hard to tell what book was actually their favorite. Quinn thought they just loved to hear the sound of anyone reading to them. Thanks to many of the guys who worked at the shop, they had a never-ending supply of children's books to read to them.

Derek finished setting up the various inks he wanted to use and then helped her get settled on the cushioned stool in front of his station, placing an overstuffed pillow in her hands. "What am I supposed to do with this?" Quinn arched one eyebrow and bit her lower lip slightly. "I mean, I thought you said the best position for this tat was for me to sit instead of lay flat on the table."

"You're supposed to wrap your arms around it, silly. That way it'll put your shoulder and back in the right position for me to draw and shade with the tat gun. You want the lettering to be straight, don't you?" He winked and kissed her on her forehead.

"Oh! Well, now the pillow makes sense."

He looked at her closely while slipping on the black latex gloves he wore while he worked. "Are you okay? You seem a mile away."

Quinn smiled and shook her head. "I'm fine, just a little distracted is all. With the twins' birthday party tonight and the thing at the club tomorrow for our anniversary, I feel a little overwhelmed. Not that I'm complaining or anything, but you know how it is when we get both the families together."

Derek chuckled as he applied the transfer paper to her left shoulder, giving him the basic outline for the tropical island design and sunrise. "Chaos is the best description. Happy chaos, just like when you first walked in here with the babies. It's not every day people get to see little ones around here, let alone the twins of two people we've all known for years. It has to be a hundred times worse when it's our families."

"Exactly. I don't think there's been a day since Stephie and Danny were born that Jake and I've had one day alone. Last night was our first 'grown up' outing."

"Well, I don't think you can count a dinner meeting with an ex-girlfriend as an outing and definitely not a date." Derek loaded the tattoo gun with the black ink as he moved his chair in front of her. "I heard it all went well for you guys though."

"It did. We learned a hell of a lot about each other, including the fact all of us have been on the Island." Derek moved back to his position behind her and started outlining the design. As with her previous tattoos, the first few moments the needles touched her skin were a bit tense, but after a minute or two, Quinn relaxed and was able to continue talking. "Julia wants to introduce us to her partner tomorrow night and then tell us all about her visit there."

"Well, after everything we've all been through over the years, I don't find it hard to believe at all that the Island existed or that the three of you were actually there. I was there myself after my accident."

"I remember. What is it with the men I love and the near-death experiences?"

"Don't know but I'm guessing it's because we're all bullheaded and it's the only way to get our attention."

"You might be on to something."

"One day you should try to see if you can make a trip back there, maybe have that date night on the beach?"

Quinn sighed. "I would love to give it a try, but I'm not sure I can do it again, let alone get there at the same time as Jake."

"Sure, you can." Brigid looked over the counter with a huge smile on her face. "Tonight would be the perfect time for it. I'll take care of the little monsters while you guys lock yourselves in your master bedroom. If you want, I can go over the basics of dream walking for both of you before you sequester yourselves."

Quinn tilted her head and smiled. "Well, even if it doesn't work, at least we will get some alone time in."

"It'll work. Stop selling yourself short. You've always been able to do it. You just had to *believe* you could."

Quinn rolled her eyes and snorted.

"Okay, I know that's a bit hokey, but it's true. Now that your memories have all come back to you both, the door is open again. Think of it as an anniversary gift from The Three."

The quiet buzz of the tattoo gun stopped as Derek took a moment to switch to a different color ink. "I agree with Brig. The timing just seems right now. Not only are we celebrating the blessings in your lives this year, you've once again helped another find their way."

He filled in a bit more on what Quinn assumed was the sunrise portion of her tattoo. It stung somewhat, and she couldn't stop from holding her breath and gritting her teeth.

"Just a few more moments with this color and we'll take a break."

Brigid looked back at the now-sleeping babies. "It appears the munchkins are way ahead of you."

Quinn laughed. "Oh, they'll be wide awake as soon as Jake is within thirty feet of the shop."

"And so will you." Derek kissed her cheek after wiping some excess ink from her back. "Now don't try to deny it. Everyone who knows you and Jake can feel the bond between you whenever you get close to each other. The two of you had that connection right from the start. Why wouldn't your kids have it, too?"

"And that's why tonight's the perfect time for the two of you to go back to the Island. Your bond has grown so strong over the last year, there's no way you won't be able to get there together and return in the morning. I'll be right there in your suite just in case, but it's not me who'll make sure you come back."

Stephanie's head popped up, and she started to look around. Daniel rolled toward the side of the playpen and pulled himself up into a standing position. Both babies gurgled and cooed just moments before Jacob and Eric strolled through the front door of the shop.

"What did we miss?" Jacob bent over and picked up both children now chattering loudly in their baby language. "You keeping Mommy distracted while Uncle Derek draws on her back?"

Derek laughed. "She's taking a short break before we finish the last of the sunrise and then the writing. Come take a look."

Jacob carried the twins in his arms easily as he made his way back to Derek's station. "Honey, your brother has outdone himself again. The colors in the sunrise are exactly as I remember them. He even captured their reflection off the water."

Quinn smiled and kissed Jacob softly. "Did you have any doubt? What do you think of the words?" She handed him the final sketch. She deliberately held off showing him the words she wanted to incorporate in the tattoo until now.

Her husband's sharp intake of breath almost made her second-guess her choice, but then the smile slowly formed on his face and in his eyes. "My Heart and Soul...Always and Forever." Jacob nodded. "They're perfect. I love you, baby doll."

She trailed her fingers along his stubbly chin and remembered the very first time he said those words to her. "I love you, too." Brigid and Derek were right. It was time to make it back to the Island, and tonight was the night Quinn vowed to do it.

* * * *

Jacob got up from the rocker to place Stephanie in the crib next to her already-snoring brother. *Just like his Mommy.* He watched them sleep, wondering at how much his life had changed over that last few years. These two held his heart hostage, and he couldn't stand being away from them for more than a few hours. How the hell was he going to handle it when they were old enough to go to school? Five years ago, having kids wasn't even a thought in his head, but now he couldn't imagine his life without them or Quinn.

His wife's arms wrap around his waist and gently pulled him away from the crib. "Come on, handsome. Brigid's got one of the baby monitors with her and will keep watch over them tonight. It's time for our dream date. Are you ready?"

"Brig made it all sound so simple. You really think we can do this again? Together this time?" He wished with all his heart they could. He yearned to go back and see the paradise that had been locked away in his memory for over ten years. He wanted to relive a piece of that even for just one night. This time they would travel there during happy times and not out of desperation to find each other.

"I want this to happen for us with all of my heart, too, honey. All the stars are aligned and ready to go according to my cousin, and I'm not about to argue with her. Come on, let's see if we can get there at sunrise and have an entire day alone in paradise."

He scooped her up into his arms as they walked down the hallway to their own bedroom. The lights were dimmed and the room filled with candles. He smelled sandalwood, vanilla, and lavender. All soothing scents to help them relax and create a peaceful, calm environment, making it easier for them to travel through the dream realm to their destination. Jacob picked up her string bikini she had placed on the bed alongside his swim trunks. "I see you thought of everything."

She shrugged. "I just did what Brigid suggested. I went with what felt right. I'm not sure if the bathing suits will make it there with us, but at least it will get us into the beach mentality."

He held her close and kissed the top of her head. "I think it's perfect. Besides, you know how much I love to see you in that bikini." Quinn giggled against his chest. "Okay, out of it, too!"

She pulled back from him and slipped her oversized T-shirt over her head and tossed it on the floor. There she stood completely naked in front of him and even more beautiful than the day he first laid eyes on her. She held his gaze and slipped her fingers under the waistband of his pajama bottoms and edged them down over his hips. "Here. Let me help you. You're wearing too many pieces of clothing for the beach."

CHAPTER 26

The Island, Present Day

A soft, balmy breeze kissed her skin as she slowly woke from her dream. Quinn inhaled deeply, filling her nose with the salty ocean air. Her eyes flew open as she sat upright in the bed. *We did it!* She turned to the empty spot in the bed next to her and her heart skipped a few beats. "Jake?"

The billowing curtains in front of the sliding glass doors parted, and there he stood, in a white satin robe, smiling. Relief washed over her, and she returned his smile. "Come on, sleepyhead, the show's about to start."

Déjà vu swept through her. "We've done this before but—"

"The first time you were here waiting for me to watch the sunrise."

Quinn nodded and slipped on the robe left for her at the end of the bed. The satin felt cool against her skin, adding a few more goose bumps. "Honey, there was another time when you were awake before me and standing out on that deck."

Jacob smiled and wrapped his arms around her. "Two years ago. I remember that now, too. Come on. Let's see if the view is just as spectacular this time around."

As the colors of the sky begin to brighten and light up the sky, they headed out toward the beach and the crashing surf. About halfway between the bungalow and the shoreline they came upon a blanket spread out on the sand in front of them with a picnic basket filled with fruit, pastries, and a tall thermos that Quinn assumed was topped off with the fabulous coffee she remembered from their last stay.

129

She looked up into his eyes and squeezed his hand tight. "You must have been up a while to get this ready."

"I wish I could take the credit for this setup, but I'm guessing maybe Danny or Pop."

Her eyes widened. "Wait. Do you think maybe Lucius did this?"

Jacob tilted his head to the side and appeared to think about it for a moment. "I don't see why not. We made it back together. This could all be his way to help us retrieve the last of our memories of this place and fulfill his promise to Fate."

Quinn allowed her robe to slip off her shoulders and to the sand as she stood on tiptoe in order to wrap her arms around his neck. "Well, I'm going to just go with it, if that's all right with you?" Jacob's robe quickly fell away, giving her the answer she wanted.

They were alone again on the Island, the place where they first fell in love long before they actually met in the real world. Quinn could hardly believe it at first, but then again after everything they had gone through to be together, why couldn't their return trip to their private paradise be real? Robes long forgotten, they held each other close as the sun rose over the horizon. Visions of Fate visiting her and asking her to choose, the blessing of their union with the birth of their children, knowing her brother Daniel's legacy lived on in Derek, and many other people made her smile through the tears blurring her vision.

"What?" Jacob nuzzled her ear softly as he brushed a few stray hairs from her forehead. "What's going on in that overactive mind of yours now?"

"I believe. For the first time in my life, I can say I believe in happily ever after. I believe love can conquer all, and I believe in the Promise of The Three." The sky suddenly burst into a medley of orange, red, and yellow, finishing with the flash of green just across the water. Quinn laughed and clapped her hands. "Thank you for giving our memories back to us!"

Jacob smiled and closed his eyes. "Yes. Thank you for letting us return one more time." He turned away from the spectacular array of colors playing out in front of them and pulled her down with him on the blanket, keeping his eyes locked with hers. "Can you feel it, baby doll? The love is so strong here. It's so—"

"Complete. It feels complete and never ending." Quinn ran her fingertips along his stubbly jawline before bringing them to his lips.

"You are my heart and soul." He kissed her fingers before she pulled them away to touch the new tattoo on his chest, gently moving along the words Derek included in the design.

Jacob's mouth found hers, tongues slowly twirling around each other, slipping, sliding, giving, and taking, leaving them both breathless with need for each other. "You are my always and forever."

Quinn's hands slipped around to the muscles along his back, nails digging in slightly as Jacob's mouth trailed along her neck to her breasts. She gasped as he took first one and then the other nipple between his teeth. She combed her fingers through his hair, loving the fact he still wore it long, just past his shoulders. The silkiness of it fascinated her but not as much as his tongue gradually snaking its way down between her legs, pausing for a moment to flick at the diamond stud in her belly button.

"Oh, Jake..." The rest of the words caught in her throat.

He looked up as he hovered over her shaved pussy. A sly grin formed on the lips she loved to kiss and have all over her body. Her pulse quickened, anticipating his next move. His tongue quickly darted out and caressed her engorged clit. Quinn's body jumped at the intimate touch and she clenched her thighs, eliciting a deep chuckle from him. "My, my, my. Aren't we a bit sensitive today."

She giggled softly. "I wouldn't call it sensitive, more like extremely responsive to my lover. You know I can't help it when we're together."

"You do the same for me, every single time." He dipped his head and latched his lips over her clit, sucking hard. She bucked against him, riding the waves of pleasure crashing through her. His fingers dug into the flesh of her ass, holding her in place as his tongue swirled rapidly a few more times around her nubbin before diving into her hot, wet folds.

Quinn's back arched as she came in his mouth, her body still quaking and quivering in response to every touch and kiss. Jacob slid up her torso, nibbling and tasting again as he made his way up back into her arms. Her own mouth hungry for his, she plunged her tongue between his lips. The scent and taste of her cum on his skin sent her desire for him skyrocketing toward another orgasm. His cock jumped against her inner thighs, teasing her even more.

She opened to him, wrapping her legs around his waist, digging her heels into his ass. "Please, baby. I need you inside me now."

He propped himself up enough to gaze deeply into her eyes as he thrust into her ever so slowly, inch by glorious inch until he filled her completely. Pausing only a moment to possess her mouth again, he pulled his cock out of her and slammed back in hard, beginning the slow buildup in speed that would send her completely over the edge once again.

* * * *

Her nails raked down his back as he buried his dick in her pussy over and over again. He couldn't get enough of her. It seemed so long since they were able to just let go and not worry about anything or anyone, just the two of them loving each other completely.

"Fuck me harder, baby." Quinn's husky words in his ear sent him careening toward his own climax. With just her voice alone, she could make him come, and that morning was no exception.

He thrust inside her cunt one last time. Her inner walls clenched hard around him, keeping him buried to the hilt while his cum shot out of his cock. Quinn clung to him as his pelvis ground into hers, his balls contracting as every last drop of his seed emptied into her.

Jacob cradled his wife in his arms as their breathing returned to normal. She traced the outline of the Island tattoo over his heart, just to the left of the center of his chest. He covered her hand with his own. "You are my everything, Quinn. I can't imagine my life without you."

"You're never going to have to. You're stuck with me now, warts and all." She kissed his chest and settled back down with her head on his shoulder.

"Warts and all, including the snoring." Jacob smiled against the top of her head, waiting for the inevitable discussion about who snored louder.

Quinn laughed. "The twins inherited that trait from the both of us. You can deny it all you want, but I have proof." She lifted her head up long enough to nip him on the chin.

"And what sort of proof might that be?" His hand slid down to settle on her lower back over the mating dragon tattoo that covered it. The pair was identical to those that covered his entire upper back.

While Quinn's dragons were in the middle of a mating dance, Jacob's dragons were in a fight to the death. At least that was the idea when he had Derek design the tattoo. Now he thought of both tattoos as depictions of the white-hot passion he and Quinn had for each other and those they loved. "You have the nanny cam set up to spy on me now?" He tweaked her nipple slightly, making her giggle again.

God, I love that sound.

She slapped his fingers away as he went in for another pinch. "Nothing that elaborate. I just recorded you with my cell phone while you slept on the couch with Steph and Danny. All three of you were pretty melodic."

"Touché. Two can play at that game you know. I have video of you snoring, too. So, I guess we'll have to call this one a draw."

Quinn sat up and reached for their robes. "A draw it is, for now." She leaned over and kissed him with her eyes wide open. "Come on, hot stuff. Let's take the picnic back up to the bungalow. We can decide what else we want to do while we're here. I'm guessing we have until sundown before we'll need to get ready to go back home."

"I'm thinking we let you recover a bit before we see what we can do with all that fruit." Jacob wiggled his eyebrows up and down.

She tossed his robe so that it covered his head, muffling his laughter. "Listen to you! Let me recover? How about you join me in the hot tub first, then we can discuss your fruit fetish."

"My fetish? You're the one who teased me with it on our first date here." He grabbed the basket as Quinn folded up the blanket. "I just followed your lead is all. Is it my fault you taste fucking fabulous after you've ingested these kinds of foods?"

She wrapped her arms around him and hugged him close enough to whisper in his ear. "The fruit has the same effect on you, too, ya know."

"So you keep telling me."

"Want me to prove it to you?" Now it was her turn to wiggle her eyebrows up and down. *Damn. She can even make that move hot as hell!*

"The only fruity cum I want to be tasting is what squirts out of you when I eat you out."

"Such vulgar language. You kiss your children with that mouth?" Quinn bit her lower lip, struggling to hide the smile that threatened to break out. Jacob loved it when she teased him with her prim-and-proper act. He knew firsthand how dirty her mouth could be, especially during sex.

Jacob nodded. "Uh-huh, and their foul-mouthed mother, too." He dodged her half-hearted punch aimed at his arm. "What? Are you denying you have a potty mouth?" He placed the basket on the deck next to the Jacuzzi before he slipped out of his robe and stepped into the hot, bubbly water.

Quinn rolled her eyes before dropping the blanket and her own robe. "No, you got me dead to rights on that point, but I am trying to be G-rated around the twins. Around you, well, that's a whole other ball game." She took his hand and let him help her settle down in the water across from him. Immediately he lifted her feet into his lap and started the massage he knew she loved. "Now you keep that up and I'll let loose with every cuss word I know. Hell, I'll even make up a few."

"You are such a tease, Mrs. Hartley."

She winked. "I'm not teasing. It's more like enticing."

"Touché."

CHAPTER 27

February 14, Las Vegas, Present Day

She watched Jacob sleeping next to her, a hint of a smile still on his face. She reached out to brush the hair off his forehead and placed her hand on his cheek. "Happy anniversary." Quinn's voice was barely a whisper, but she knew he heard her clearly.

His hand slid up her thigh to rest in the middle of her back before he pulled her close to his body. Jacob wrapped both arms around her snuggly and rested his forehead against hers before opening his deep-blue eyes. "Happy anniversary to you, too."

"What's the last thing you remember about the Island?" Quinn was curious if his memories were the same as hers or if she dreamt the whole thing.

"I remember dancing with you on the beach after the steak dinner we prepared together this time." He winked at her and smiled. "We decided to have the same meal we were to have the very first night we spent together since we already got the sex out of the way."

Quinn giggled. "Yeah, well this time we are an old married couple, so we can have our dessert before dinner if we damn well please." She snuggled up closer to him and kissed his neck. "What else do you remember?"

"I remember telling you if we never get to visit the Island again I was happy with that because each and every day here with you in the real world is like living in paradise."

She nodded. "Yep. We were there together. It wasn't a dream."

He tilted his head back a bit to look into her eyes. "You doubted it?"

"For a moment when I first woke up, I did. Everything looked exactly as we left it here when we fell asleep. I wasn't sure if it actually worked or not, but it really didn't matter. It was a beautiful gift even if it was a dream. I was just hoping that you got to experience it, too."

"Every single moment of it, baby doll. It's something I'll never forget."

Before Quinn had a chance to answer, the baby monitor came to life. First Stephanie and then Danny began their morning ritual of cooing and giggling. Through all the nonsense sounds came a clear "mum" followed quickly by "dah." Jacob's eyes widened, but Quinn silenced him with a finger over his lips. Sure enough, the twins kept up the short words, calling for them. "Well, looks like the munchkins want to get in on the celebrating again today."

"It is their first birthday after all." Jacob rolled onto his back as Quinn got up out of bed and slipped her T-shirt back on. "I guess since they crashed our wedding, they feel the need to take over our anniversary, too, not that I'm complaining. I got an entire night alone with you in our beach hideaway. What more can a guy ask for?"

Quinn smiled. "Last night was perfect, but I do have a few more surprises in store for you today."

He got up quickly from the bed and scooped her into his arms before she even registered he moved. "Good. I have another one for you, too, and it's a doozy." He kissed her nose and then possessed her lips, sucking on her tongue. "But you'll have to wait until the party tonight to get it. You think you can handle the wait?"

Her answer was drowned out by two little ones getting loud enough to wake the casino. "How about you help me get them ready to spend the day with our families and stop wondering if I can wait for your surprise or not."

"Don't you want even a small hint?" Quinn nearly laughed at the surprised look on his face, but she held her tongue and shook her head while she watched him slip into his pajama bottoms. "Seriously? You hate surprises, and you always badger the hell out of me to give you clues when I try to surprise you with anything. What gives?"

Quinn opened their bedroom door and walked quickly down the hall toward the guest room that served as the nursery. Jacob nearly collided with Brigid trying to keep up with her. "Don't mind him, cousin. He's trying to get me to beg for clues about some surprise he's got planned for me."

Brigid put her hands up in the air in mock surrender and excused herself to go start breakfast for everyone. Jacob caught up to Quinn at the crib. Both babies squealed with delight to see them. "Now which one of you called for your poppy?" Jacob reached out, and Danny practically jumped into his arms while Stephanie reached for Quinn. "Happy first birthday, Dan the Man."

Stephanie clapped her little hands together and giggled as only a toddler can. Quinn laughed along with her. "Happy birthday to you, too, my little princess." She couldn't believe how much both toddlers had grown in the year. It seemed just like yesterday when she found out she was pregnant after many years of thinking she was unable to conceive. Her eyes filled with happy tears, and she let them fall down her cheeks freely.

"Honey, why're you crying?"

"I'm just so happy. We have each other and our children. Everything is as it should be."

"Damn." Jacob smiled and shook his head.

"What did I say?"

"Without even trying, you are going to get me to tell you my surprise."

Quinn shook her head. "No, really, I can wait until you're ready to tell me." She really was trying to wait him out this time and didn't want him to surprise her with anything until the moment he planned to do it.

"I'm ready to tell you now. It's the perfect time." She stopped pulling out the clothes for the twins and waited for him to spill it. "Eric and I looked at a few properties in Henderson yesterday, and I found the perfect house. It has a huge backyard that's perfect for a pool when the kids are bigger. There's also a park nearby, and the schools…" Jacob stopped talking and stared at her. "Honey?"

"You want to move to Nevada? I thought you liked living in California? What about your job with the specialty center? You just got that program up and running."

Relief washed over his face. "Is that what you're worried about? My job? Baby doll, the work on the new emergency veterinary hospital can go much faster if you are here to supervise it. Besides, the animal rehab facility in California will do just fine without me. Steve's asked me to help set up one here, too. I'll be consulting on that project while I work in the new sports rehab facility at UNLV.

They've asked me to come back as part of the teaching staff. I haven't given any of them firm answers. I wanted to talk to you first and then we could decide as a family."

Quinn's heart overflowed with love for her husband. "Babe, you moved to San Francisco to be with me without even batting an eye eighteen months ago. Now you've not only found us a new home to be closer to one of my new hospitals, you've found the job of your dreams. I don't think there's anything left to discuss." She smiled and hugged him as tight as she could with both babies between them.

"I guess we better get a move on. We've got a lot to do today before the party at the club tonight." He kissed her softly and tossed his son up in the air. "What do you say, Danny? Are you happy about moving to Vegas?" Squeals of laughter filled the nursery.

Quinn sat down in the rocker to start nursing Stephanie while Jacob bathed Daniel. *Yep. Everything is as it's supposed to be. Wait until he hears about my surprise!*

* * * *

Steve really outdid himself. Saints and Sinners was filled to capacity with all their friends and family celebrating their anniversary and the plans for the renovations of the club. Jacob had an inkling Steve wasn't all that surprised by their decision to move to Henderson. Not much happened in and around Vegas that he didn't know about. That was okay with him. Jacob liked having someone so influential on his side instead of competing for Quinn's affections. That part of their lives was ancient history, and Steve had become one of his closest friends, not to mention the godfather to his children.

Quinn floated around the room in her red off-the-shoulder evening gown, greeting everyone and looking as hot as ever. The dress brought back all sorts of memories of the night they first met right on the dance floor in front of him. While the music changed to a slow number, Jacob kept his eyes glued on Quinn as she excused herself from a group of her friends waiting at the bar for one of his brother Eric's famous margaritas.

She searched the room casually, smiling at those who greeted her. She appeared to be a lady on a mission to find her dance partner. He couldn't let her wait any longer and moved through the crowd toward her. As his eyes locked with hers, that telltale sensation hit him fast and hard. Once again, he was thunderstruck. Thankfully this time he wasn't rooted to the spot and he made it to her side without falling on his face.

"Can I have this dance?"

She gifted him with her radiant smile. Not that she needed anything to brighten her disposition. She positively glowed and appeared even more beautiful than on their wedding day. Right on cue, the DJ transitioned to the next song. It was the one they first danced to as husband and wife, "Unchained Melody."

"I thought you'd never ask."

She molded against his body easily. With the help of her favorite four-inch stilettos, Quinn now stood nearly eye to eye with him. Jacob wanted nothing more than to get lost in her blue-green eyes tonight and every night. He couldn't think of one thing that would make this night any more special.

"You look like you're a million miles away."

"Sorry. I was just thinking that this anniversary couldn't be any better. Not only did we have our alone time on a secluded island, we put an offer on a new home, moved forward with our dream jobs, celebrated it all with just about all of the Hartley and Quartermarsh clans, and now I get to dance with the love of my life. I can't ask for anything more."

"I still have one more surprise for you that just may put you over the top."

Jacob raised his eyebrow and guided her into a dip at the end of the song. "What else could possibly make this day more memorable?" He eased her back up to gaze into her eyes, still holding her in his arms in the middle of the dance floor.

"Steph and Danny are going to have a new sibling around the end of August."

"Another baby? Are you sure?" He searched her face to gauge what she was thinking. Her kilowatt smile slowly came back into view. Jacob let go of the air he had held in his lungs. He hadn't realized he wasn't breathing until that moment.

"I took an at-home test and then went in to see the doctor last week. I've been dying to tell you about our new addition but wanted to surprise you with it tonight. It's been so hard keeping it a secret, and I nearly spilled it in Steve's office the other day." She placed both hands on either side of his face and made him look into her eyes. "We're going to have the family we've always dreamed of together. Is that okay with you? You look a bit pale."

Jacob laughed, picked her up off her feet, and twirled her around. "You better believe it's okay with me!"

Steve came up to them in the middle of the dance floor with a microphone. "Let me guess. Quinn finally told you about your big surprise?"

Jacob nodded. "You knew? All this time you knew and didn't tell me?"

He handed Jacob the microphone and shook his head. "It was her news to tell. There was no way in hell I was going to get in the middle of that. You know how she is!"

Quinn smacked Steve's arm. "Hey! Stop talking about me as if I'm not in the room."

One voice boomed out over the club. "Will somebody tell us what's going on?" It was Jacob's brother still behind the bar sans tuxedo jacket, with his sleeves rolled up. "I've got thirsty people here wanting their margaritas."

Jacob turned on the microphone and looked out at all the friends and family gathered around them and cleared his throat. "Most of you know our story. I thought the happiest day of my life was when Quinn agreed to be my wife, then we found out we were expecting the twins. Our wedding day wasn't your run-of-the-mill celebration either. Not only did we get to pledge our love for each other before all of you, Stephanie and Danny decided they wanted to be part of the party, too. Now here we are, one year later, and my cup runneth over." Tears filled his eyes, and Jacob had to take a moment to collect his composure before he continued. Quinn held his hand tightly and kissed his cheek, giving him the final boost he needed. "We're having another baby."

Cheers and applause erupted, and they were immediately surrounded by everyone congratulating them. Quinn stayed by his side and never let go of his hand through it all. They'd come full circle back to the place where it all began. Everything was indeed as it should be. They were together, now and forever.

THE END

ABOUT THE AUTHOR

As far back as I can remember I have had two dreams: become a veterinarian and a world-famous author. So far, I achieved the first one and have enjoyed a wonderful career as a small-animal veterinarian. But something has always been missing. I've never stopped writing; that has never been an issue. The problem was getting up the nerve to actually finish one of my novels and submit it to a publisher. What a scary thought to send a stranger something I had poured my heart into. Would they like it? Would they see the characters the way I saw them in my head? Writing *For the Love of Quinn* was like giving birth to my first child. I had to let my characters go to see if they would take off, and boy have they ever!

Jacob and Quinn's story is far from over. With this revised addition, they shared more of their world. While their journey to find each other has come to an end, their love continues to live on. They'll pop in from time to time to check in with their friends and family in the next books in the Now and Forever series. They have their happily ever after, and now it's time for the others to find theirs, too!

Having grown up in Michigan and now living in the Pacific Northwest, I have had the privilege to experience life in a small town and a big city. Everyone who I've met along the way has influenced my writing in one way or another. Their experiences as well as my own help make up the characters that I hold near and dear to my heart. Helping them find the loves of their lives as well as fulfilling a few fantasies along the way is just frosting on the cake.

You can find me on Twitter, Facebook, Pinterest and my website authortammydenningsmaggy.com. I love to hear from you!

Bonus Material: Two chapters from

Bound in Paradise
by Tammy Dennings Maggy
© 2014

Chapter 1

Twenty-five years ago, Los Angeles, California

This is what I've worked so hard for! I finally get my chance to show off my work to people who'll appreciate it.

Julia smiled, hung back, and allowed the scene before her to burn into her mind. Among those who adored her work were a few very vocal patrons who absolutely hated it. She smiled. Those were the raw, passionate responses she craved to bring out in people, whether with her art or with her body. The rush of excitement that flooded her now put her nerves on edge and primed for one more touch to send her completely over the top. To her, there was no other feeling like it in the world, other than a run of full body orgasms, which had been in short supply for her lately because of her preparations for the gallery showing.

The theme of the evening had grabbed her attention as soon as she'd heard about it from one of her lovers. Sexual fantasy encompassed such a wide variety of heat levels. Fortunately for Julia, nearly all the other artists concentrated on the vanilla sort. She dove head on into the world of BDSM—her world. The one in which she thrived. Her pieces represented the concept of sublime submission of slaves to their Masters, and to lovers in general.

The advance promotions of her collection had created quite a stir and on opening night the gallery had been packed—thanks to her.

The other artists benefited as well. The extra hoopla her art elicited had resulted in more sales of their work, too. So far it had been a mutually beneficial collaboration. Tonight was the second night of her exhibition and her excitement continued to build with each passing moment. The butterflies in her stomach flew to attention as another group crowded around her section of the floor. One couple, in particular, caught her eye. She'd been waiting for her chance to meet them as soon as the doorman had told her they'd arrived.

The tall, model thin red-headed beauty gasped in delight as her fingers traced over one of Julia's sculptures. "Darling, will you look at this detail! I've never seen anyone capture this anywhere. I can feel this sub's complete surrender."

"I agree. We have to have this one, too. Let's see. That one will bring us up to two sculptures to go with the three paintings we've tagged. This is turning into one expensive outing!"

The woman pouted. "You promised I could have anything I wanted tonight. Besides, you were the one to jump on the last piece."

He laughed. "I'd gladly take home every single one of them if we could."

Julia approached and smiled. "That can be arranged."

He turned toward her and flashed a smile that nearly knocked Julia off her feet. He oozed sex and control.

Now here's a Dom who's comfortable in his own skin and in control of all around him. Where can I find one like him?

"Ms. Santos! We were hoping to meet you tonight. Your art has created quite the buzz around town."

"Mr. and Mrs. Mitchell, I've heard so much about you. The gallery owner said you'd placed orders for a few of my pieces as soon as you received your invitation. Of course, I'd be here in person to thank you for your interest in my work. Please. Call me Julia."

"As long as you drop the Mr. and Mrs. stuff. This is my wife, Rita and I'm Jarrod."

She shook his hand and smiled. "Deal. This is my first showing, so please forgive me if I seem out of sorts. I've had to pinch myself a few times to be sure I'm not dreaming."

His deep, baritone laughter rang out. "I assure you. This is no dream. We have a large collection of BDSM art and I have to say yours is the most lifelike. I've not seen a more accurate portrayal of our lifestyle. None of our community has."

She laughed. "I find that hard to believe. The gallery is filled with beautiful creations."

Rita shook her head. "Nothing like yours."

"I'm flattered you think so highly of my work, especially since you purchased a third of my showing." She reached for Rita's hands and squeezed them.

Jarrod nodded. "The pleasure is all ours. We're planning a small gathering of our friends to show off our purchases. We'd love it if you'd agree to be our guest of honor. I noticed in the program you're taking commissions. Our party could help drum up more business for you. No pressure of course." He winked and placed his arm around Rita's waist.

The gesture struck a chord deep inside her. She longed to have a partner who treated her with dignity and respect in public but had complete control in private. She sensed that was the case between the Mitchells. There was no doubt in her mind they were a couple comfortable in their own skins and in their relationship. Drawn to their chemistry, Julia resisted the urge to jump up and down with joy at their invitation. Instead, she tilted her head to the side and bit her lip. "I'll have to check my schedule, but I would love any chance to show off my work."

Jarrod clapped his hands and rubbed them together. "It's settled then. We'll hash out the details and then get with you about potential dates that fit both of our schedules."

Rita slipped her arm through his and leaned in conspiratorially. "I'd like to hire you to create something just for us…for our private collection."

He patted her hand. "Excellent proposition, pet. What do you say, Julia?"

"I think it's a fabulous idea. To get the most accurate scene, I'll want to use the two of you as models." She lifted her eyebrows and waited to see how they would react to her declaration.

"You mean in full on play mode?" Rita's eyes widened and a soft blush tainted her cheeks.

She nodded. "If you want the same realism portrayed in these pieces, you'll have to agree to be the subjects."

"Sounds exciting. We're in." Jarrod's smile lit up his face again.

Rita bounced on the balls of her feet and appeared to be trying to keep from jumping up and down like a schoolgirl. "Our schedules are wide open for the next few months. You pick the day and time and we'll be there—props, crops, and all!"

She laughed. "Perfect. How about you come by my studio tomorrow at ten and we'll get started. Here's the address. I can't wait to have you model for me." She reached into the cleft between her breasts and pulled out one of her business cards.

Rita's slow seductive smile took Julia's breath away. She bit her lip again as Rita slipped the card into her small clutch. The Mitchells then excused themselves and promised to be at her studio as directed.

She admired the ease with which the couple discussed their sexuality. Sure it was in a joking manner, but there was no question in her mind Jarrod was the dominant. Rita's mannerisms were not what some Doms expected from their subs in public. Where Rita exuded poise, strength, and self-confidence while deferring to Jarrod, other subs would've demonstrated complete subservience—never speaking unless given permission to do so. While this was all well and good for them, it wasn't what she craved. She's longed for the same kind of relationship since she first realized her sexual tendencies drifted toward the more taboo and risqué.

She desired a partner strong enough and confident enough in their relationship they would allow her to be wild and free, and trust her to give over complete control to them in private. Meeting the Mitchells renewed her hope she would find her perfect match one day. Maybe the couple would help her take the first steps in that direction.

This is exactly what I'd hoped would happen with this showing. Not only did I sell several pieces, I've met two kindred spirits. Tomorrow will be an experience they'll never forget. In the end, they'll have something to remind them of it every time they look at it. Maybe they'll formally introduce me to a few more in the lifestyle. I'm really getting tired of the same old crowd at the clubs.

In her mind, anything would be better than the diner crowd she'd dealt with the first three years she'd lived in California. On her sixteenth birthday, she'd walked out of the hell her parents had created. Years of mental and sexual abuse had been all she'd ever known and had come to think of as normal. She never knew anything different. She didn't have any friends in school and had kept to herself.

Her only safe haven had been with her maternal grandmother. Those times had been the only happy moments she remembered. When questioned, she'd denied the abuse because she'd feared her stepfather would follow through with his threats to kill the only person who'd ever shown her love and kindness.

Her grandmother had orchestrated her escape. She'd made her promise to run as far as she could and never, ever come back—no matter what happened. The woman had provided Julia with a purse full of money and a list of names of people she could trust to keep her safe.

After shedding many tears, Julia had agreed. The first name on her list had been her great aunt and grandmother's sister. She'd helped her change her name and start fresh with a job at the local diner during the day and one with the movie theater at night. At sixteen, she hadn't been required by law to go to school, and with her work schedule, she'd had very little time for it. However, after settling into her routine, she did complete her course work to get her diploma.

Once she'd turned eighteen and saved enough money, she had moved out on her own. Her aunt had wished her well and promised to be there if she ever needed anyone again. No matter how much she wanted to reach out to her aunt and grandmother, she kept her vow and never looked back.

Now after three more years, and countless hours painting, sculpting and honing her craft, she'd finally arrived. Exhibiting her work boosted her confidence enough to finally trust in her ability to create anything her clients desired. It had been at another artist's exhibit where she'd discovered the local BDSM crowd and art world. The painter's work was good, but Julia had known she could do much better and had made it her mission to show the world just what she could do.

Through connections with one of her art teachers and lovers, she had been introduced to several collectors interested in her genre of sexually taboo art. Her sketches alone won them over and it's how she had been invited to display her work in the gallery today.

Garrett James, the gallery owner approached and pulled her out of reminiscing. He kissed her on both cheeks. "Sweetheart, you are a hit! I have an entire log full of contacts begging for more from you.

From the looks of things, I'd say you'll have enough commissions to keep you busy in your studio for the next three or four years."

"Stop it." Her cheeks burned in response to his gushing.

"No. No. It's true. The Mitchells grabbed a stack of your cards and they have clout with many other collectors and in the local art scene. If you win them over, you are guaranteed a spot with all the galleries. You'll be so inundated with invitations that you'll need an assistant to sort them all out. Trust me. You're our new 'it' girl. Please say you'll do another exhibit with me. I can't bear to think you and your work will be out of my gallery in the blink of an eye."

She laughed at his melodramatic pleas. "Of course. I'd love to do another showing. Everyone here has inspired me. I've been sketching a few of my ideas down while they're still fresh in my mind. What do you think?"

She handed him her sketchbook and held her breath.

He whistled. "These drawings alone would make a fantastic showing. Keep these safe, my love."

"I have them locked up when not in my hands."

"Good idea." He leaned and whispered in her ear. "You have talent I haven't seen come through this town in over a decade. Don't ever sell yourself short."

She hugged him and hid the tears. Never had anyone encouraged her like this, except her grandmother. Garret reminded Julia so much of her. In fact, if he hadn't been gay, she would've introduced him to her grandmother hoping for a love match. Maybe one day they'd be able to meet. For now, there was no way she would be able to risk any contact with anyone from her past. She would lose everything she'd worked so hard to achieve. The fear of others finding out what her mother forced her to do for years squashed any urge she had to see her grandmother out of her head.

* * * *

Chapter 2

Julia stood in front of the antique mirror in the dressing room and admired Rita's handiwork. She'd piled her hair on top of her head expertly, leaving several longer curls and tendrils to fall down her neck and shoulders. She ran her hands down the curve hugging patent leather mini dress and smiled. *Sexy but still leaves something to the imagination—okay, not much but it's how the game is played.*

"I have one more thing to complete the look." Rita handed her a blue velvet jewelry box.

"What's this?" She opened the lid and gasped. Inside was a long thin silver necklace like the one Rita had worn during their modeling sessions.

"Let me help you with it." Rita carefully looped the chain over her head and around her neck three times and let the rest dangle between the cleft between her breasts.

She turned back toward the mirror and smiled. "It's beautiful. Thank you."

"The chain will show you're a submissive looking for a dominant for more than just an occasional play party. Jarrod and I will watch over you. If you feel uncomfortable at all and need us to intervene, start playing with the chain. We'll come to your rescue." She winked and hugged her.

Julia smiled. "Will do. Jarrod mentioned he wanted to introduce me to one of your friends, but she may not be able to arrive until halfway through the party."

Rita nodded. "That's right. Carmen and Jarrod go way back. In fact, he was her sub at one time. They enjoyed each other for a time, but she realized he was more of a Dom and helped to bring that out. She's the one who introduced us to each other and now I hope we can return the favor by bringing the two of *you* together. She works such long hours at the hospital and has had very little time to socialize let alone devote herself to any new sub. She's been promoted to the head of her department and we thought our party was the perfect place for her to celebrate the accomplishment."

"I understand working nonstop to achieve your goals. How did you get her to say accept your invitation?"

Rita giggled. "We hounded her day and night and wouldn't take no for an answer. All work and no play makes for a very dull Carmen, and we can't have that. Plus, we've told her all about your artwork and she's excited to see it for herself."

"Well, at least we'll have something to talk about. I'm as devoted to my career as she is. Ask me about my work and I'll talk your ear off!"

Rita hugged her again. "You'll do fine. Relax and be yourself. The Power of the Submissive painting is the center of the display. Carmen will be drawn to it as we were in the gallery. I loved the subtle color and lighting you used to showcase the bound and collared submissive kneeling in front of her Dom. Only his hand was in the scene, but I could still feel his control over her. I couldn't tear my eyes away from it in the gallery. The overall image you portrayed is highly erotic, but the look of pure serenity on the sub's face captivated me. You captured the D/s relationship perfectly and managed to relay your desire to have the same."

She blushed. *Oh my God! She gets it. She saw the hidden message.* "Thank you. You and Jarrod are the only ones who've picked up on my plea in the painting."

"Trust me. Carmen will see it, too. Let's get you set up in the dungeon. Jarrod intentionally positioned the painting so the attendees see that first before they're able to lay eyes on you. You've built up your reputation as the dark and mysterious artist. Now we'll help you capitalize on that in order to bring you more business and hopefully find what you desire in a relationship or two."

"Since the gallery exhibit, my phone hasn't stopped ringing. There isn't enough time in my day to get to all of them. It's all happening so fast but I'm enjoying every single minute of it."

"As you should. You deserve all the attention. You're the talk of our BDSM community and everyone wants a chance to meet you. We had people beg to be invited here tonight and had to turn many away. While the majority of tonight's guests will be friendly and gracious, there is one who'll try to monopolize your time and attention away from anyone else who may be interested in you. I don't want to tell you who to hang out with tonight, but Viktor should come with a warning label attached to him."

"That bad?"

"More of an egomaniac, but there are subs who fight to be with him. Personally, he makes my skin crawl."

"I'll keep that in mind. I'm usually good at avoiding the creeps. I had a lot of practice when I worked the late shift at the diner."

"Those days are over for you, but there will always be a shit to deal with in your life. For tonight, remember to play with your chain if you need help. We have others around the playroom whose only job is to ensure everyone's safety. They'll intervene if Jarrod or I can't get to you fast enough."

She nodded and then followed as she led the way to the dungeon playroom Jarrod had set up in their basement. Her heels echoed throughout the room as she made her way down the wooden steps. She created a mental checklist of where to find everything as she walked around. The bar area had been set up on the ground floor in order to make room for the various stations in the basement. Many of her favorite things were represented from wax play to flogging. Across from her painting, Jarrod had set up a lounge area with several couches and other cushioned chairs. This would be where she and the other new members would hold court and hopefully find matchups.

Wow! They've gone all out for this gathering. The only other parties I've attended have been held in hotel rooms with little or no fanfare other than a keg and bowl of condoms on the table. Calm yourself. This isn't a frat party. This is the big league and it's what you've always wanted.

Now let's see if I can pull this off and find the dominant I need to bring out the best of me.

* * * *

Bound in Paradise and *The Surrender of Julia (Now and Forever 3)* are available now through all major electronic book outlets.

www.ingramcontent.com/pod-product-compliance
Lightning Source LLC
Chambersburg PA
CBHW051949170626
46808CB00007B/2540